Digging
FOR
Victory

Cathy Faulkner

Firefly

First published in 2023 by Firefly Press
25 Gabalfa Road, Llandaff North, Cardiff, CF14 2JJ

www.fireflypress.co.uk
Copyright © Cathy Faulkner 2023
Cover illustration copyright © Harry Goldhawk 2023

A CIP catalogue record of this book is available
from the British Library.
ISBN 9781915444110

This book has been published with the support of
the Books Council of Wales.

Typeset by Elaine Sharples and Becka Moor

Printed and bound in Great Britain by
CPI Group (UK) Ltd, Croydon, CR0 4YY

MIX
Paper | Supporting
responsible forestry
FSC
www.fsc.org   FSC® C171272

To Duncan Fraser, an inspirational teacher who
first sowed the seed.

Tuesday 3rd December 1940

Ralph's going off to be a hero.
    It's official.
He got his papers this morning –
Two-Six-Six squadron are expecting him.

Ralph's my brother, just in case you didn't know.

Ralph,
who, until not so long ago,
would sometimes play hide   and
                seek.
Not that it would ever take me long to find him
    (and then he'd pretend he wasn't even playing
    and that made me feel daft).

Ralph,
who told me the difference
between Spitfires and Hurricanes,
Wellingtons and Halifaxes,
but missed the very first actual Spitfire *flying over* the village
    (and then claimed he was the first to see it).

Ralph,
who's won the heart
of practically every girl in the village
    (apart from Mary Smith
    who will always hate him),

but who's never once won a school prize.
>   (The ones *I've* won for coming first in tests
>   don't count, he says,
>   since he gave me all the answers –
>   which isn't true anyway.)

Ralph,
who's always made me look second best,
even though I'm not.

Ralph, Mother says
>   (whilst brushing away a tear),
wouldn't want us to be sad –
we're to learn to be strong,
keep our chins up
and most of all,
FEEL PROUD.

The thing is,
        if I'm honest,
I don't actually feel sad and,
        even though I'm just his little sister,
I'm already strong.

And there's no way I'm
ever
EVER
putting my chin up
and feeling proud
until

I

am the hero.

Tuesday 17th December 1940

Can you help me carry Ralph's things down to the cellar,
Mother says,

    in her that's-what-you're-going-to-do-anyway kind of way.
Why? I ask. *He'll be back before long –*
he said he'll visit us as soon as he's got leave,
    didn't he?

Mother sighs.
We don't know when that'll be,
and now that he's really flown the nest
    for the good of the country,
it's time that we play our part too.

I wrinkle my face up.
What do you mean?

I mean, Bonnie,
that Father and I
have applied to have someone billeted here,
so now we can all look forward to someone else coming to stay.

So Ralph gets to fly away on an adventure
and we have a stranger coming to stay
(not that I was ever asked about it).
How exactly is that us playing a part in the war effort?

Boxing up Ralph's childhood –

his hard-won marbles
      (that he never let me play with),
the prize conker
      (which I know *I* found),
and badly-painted tin soldiers
      (in all the wrong colours) –
is the only part I get to play.

I dig out Grandfather's old zoetrope from under Ralph's bed –
so that's where it's been!
It's been years since we've played with it –
Ralph told Mother I'd lost it
(and, as usual, I took the blame).
I'm taking this to *my* room.

  I   place it in the middle of my windowsill.
    Rising from its polished wooden base,
      the round metal drum looks almost
        lamp – like, but upside – down with
        slits   cut   round   the   side.
          I   spin   it   really   hard,
               looking
               through
                 one
                  of
                 the
               gaps
and wonder (as I've always done) exactly how the drawings on
    the inside seem to merge into one moving picture.

                    I watch them as they chase each other
                                    round
                                            and
                                                    round
                                            and
                                    round.

They're faded now and covered in dust,
but they're just as I remember them:

the eagle
        takes off
                and soars
                        time and
                                time again,
                                        leaving the chicken
                                always
                                scratching
                        pathetically
        at the ground
below.

As I carry
    the boxes and trunks
        down to their new home
            in the cold, cobwebbed cellar,
                I wonder who might soon be moving their things in.

I hope it's someone nice
  like Barbara Robinson
    who arrived from Bristol
    with her gas mask and trunk
    and was billeted with Carol
      (my best friend in the whole world)
    last September.

Another Nancy Edwards
    (who arrived on the same train
    in her pigtails and pinafore)
  would be all right too
    (although I still don't believe
        what she said about
    never having seen a cow before.
  I'm sure she's lying).

Even a Betty Sanders
    (who talks for all three of them)
  wouldn't be too bad,
  just as long as
  she doesn't EVER say
  that things are backward here.
  I've heard that far too much already.

Or perhaps –
    now here's an idea –
  it might be one of those land girls
  who helps out on farms.

Mr Brown
    (that's our closest neighbour)
has requested some, you know,
now that his farmhands have gone off to fight.
    (He's got a lot on his plate at the moment,
      what with being in the Home Guard and all.)
I bet their trunks would be full of lipstick and pretty dresses,
stockings and high heels.
A land girl might curl my hair
and give me lovely things
just like a kind big sister.
How jealous the girls at school would be!

Yes, by the time Ralph's room is empty,
the memories boxed up
and the dust swept away,

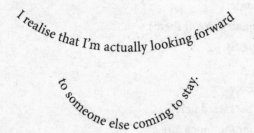

Just so long as that someone
    isn't a boy.

Thursday 2nd January 1941

No, it's not a boy,
Mother says,
as I fix the newspaper paper chain
that's given up decorating our sitting room.

Thank goodness for that.
I don't want someone who'll tease me
and call me names
and snigger like they do at school.
I want someone like Carol:
        a girl I can talk to at midnight
who'll understand me,
who'll share secrets
        (and lemon sherbets),
be like the sister I never had
and who won't ever go off and join in the action,
leaving me feeling
second best.

No, it's not a boy,
Mother repeats.
        It's a Mr Fisher.

The chain comes apart in my hands.
That can't be right! I cry.
Why on earth would a Mr Fisher
need to stay on a dairy farm
in the middle of nowhere?

He can't be a farmhand –

>they've already left to fight and only land girls are sent to
>help now.

And if he were a farmer and allowed to stay,

>why, he'd have his own farm and wouldn't be billeted here.

We don't need another doctor –

>Dr Bovingdon's busy but I'm sure he can manage now that
>half the village have gone.

A teacher perhaps?

>But the evacuees brought their own Miss Jones with them
>when they came on the train from Bristol.

Someone from the Home Guard?

>Mr Brown has that all covered what with his whole team
>of grandfathers who watch out for invaders (and they've
>hardly been run off their feet).

Maybe a new warden?

>But Revd Collins, our vicar, loves that job, and although
>he's almost as ancient as the church itself, I don't think
>anything will stop him shouting, *Put that light out!*

And if he were in the forces—

>he'd either be fighting abroad or based at RAF Oakmoor
>just ten miles north of here.

What I hope more than anything
is that he isn't another conchie like Mr Howard,

>sent here to do the jobs that no one else wants to do
>all because he has some strange belief
>and refuses to help our boys fight.
>Having one of those in the house just doesn't bear

thinking about –
the boys at school would have a reason to call me names
then.

I scrunch the remains of the paper chain
tightly into a ball
and throw it into the wastepaper basket.

But Mr Howard wasn't billeted with anyone
even though he's working for Mr Brown.
He lives in his own caravan.
Thank goodness.
Maybe all conchies do.

Mother turns the letter
over
and
over
in her hands
as if looking for the answer to my question.

It must be a mistake.

Friday 3rd January 1941

But when I open the door the very next morning
and see the scrawny RAF officer standing ankle-deep in snow,
I know it's for real.
Not a conchie,
but a man, all the same.

And everything inside turns cold.

Mr Fisher?
Mother asks, untying her apron.
He holds out his hand and gives a quick nod
but his face looks as frosty as the frozen fields behind him.

Come in, come in!
Mother shuts the door, hurriedly puts another log on the fire
and the kettle on the stove.

But the cold has come in now.

And, somehow, I think it's here to stay.

Mr Fisher's cold expression
doesn't thaw as he stands

s
t
i
f
f
l
y
by the fire.
He has a faraway look in his ice-blue eyes
and when he stares into his tea
without drinking,
it's clear he'd rather be somewhere else;
doing something different,
with people who aren't us.

Mother chatters and fusses
like she does around Father
when he comes in out of the snow.
But, unlike Father,
he simply nods,
and barely opens his mouth to speak.

And when he does,
his crotchety voice
seems to speak from

miles away.

When Mother takes the tea tray back to the kitchen,
I try to be polite and tell him about Ralph:
how he's going to be a hero of the skies at just nineteen
(I think it might be of interest, him being RAF and all),
but the way he says
    Is that so,
doesn't sound like a question at all.
He stops listening altogether,
and just looks
        out of
           the window.

I really don't like this Mr Fisher.
And I wish he were somewhere else too,
doing something different,
with people who aren't us.

And what on earth is he doing here anyway?

Bonnie,
says Mother, later in the day,
you're to be polite to Mr Fisher
and show him respect.

We've got to make him feel at home –
he'll be eating with us at our table.
You're to keep quiet outside his room
And give him no reason to grumble.

You're to offer him food before you take yours
and accept if it means having less.
You're to keep your belongings up in your room
and refrain from making a mess.

From now on, his is the chair by the fire
and he's to read any books of his choosing.
You're to make tea on Saturdays at half past ten
and polish his shoes every evening.

Oh, and under absolutely no circumstances whatsoever
        are you to ask him ANY questions.
Is that understood?

Not understood.
Not understood.
Not understood in the slightest.

How can that horrible old man
just arrive in our house
and expect us to make it his home?

Like a cuckoo,
he's taken over the nest
that Ralph has only just flown.

And like put-upon birds,
we are expected to feed him
    and show him kindness
so that he can get on
    with whatever it is that he does.

And what is that anyway?
Why is he here?
Why isn't he playing his part?

There's nothing for an officer to do on this farm.

Especially not an unsmiling one.

Not understood.
Not understood.
Not understood in the slightest.

Saturday 4th January 1941

Bonnie,
 says Mother,
  on the way to the village shop
 the very next day,
Your father and I have been talking.
What with Ralph gone –
not to mention the farmhands –
and another mouth to feed,
I'm going to have to ask you
to take on something very important.

 Oh?
I pull the loose thread on my mitten.

You see, I'll have to help your father a lot more
out in the fields with the cows.
We've all got to play our part, you know.

 Oh?
I drag my heels through the slush.
Ah! There you go, Bonnie,
she says as we turn the corner,
pointing at the poster that old Mrs Clarke
is straightening in the post-office window:

  over the top of a perfectly round cauliflower
  a lady smiles.

DIG FOR VICTORY

the poster says.

I'm not sure why Mother is showing me this.
She already grows our own vegetables.
She's been doing it ever since I can remember.

And then I realise just what she means.

I dig my mittened hands into my pocket
and dig my heels in.

I don't want to dig for victory,
I want to fight for it.

———

Standing at Mrs Barker's counter there are four girls
I've not seen before,
but their brown hats, coats and breeches
and badges of gold and green
tell me that they must be the new land girls
come to help out on Mr Brown's farm.

Mrs Barker examines their ration books,
grudgingly stamps each one
then takes off her glasses
and folds her arms tightly over her enormous chest.
Just because you're entitled to extra food,

18

doesn't mean it'll always be available,
she grumbles.
There's enough mouths to feed
in this 'ere village as it is.

Bloomin' townies,
she mutters under her breath
as the land girls step out into the snow
and the bell above the door jangles   a cheery goodbye.

Fat lot of good they'll be on a farm –
not an ounce of muscle between 'em.

Just trying to do their bit, I suppose,
Mother replies politely.

Huh!
They'd do it far better in a factory
or working the telephones –
they'll never replace our boys.

Mrs Barker is still grumbling to herself
as she disappears into the dark, dusty storeroom out the back
to find Mother some seed potatoes.
Three weeks, I'll give 'em –
you mark my words.
Three weeks.

The land girls are still on the village green
as we say goodbye to Mrs Barker and step out into the cold.
The four of them are squealing with delight
and stumbling backwards in the snow
        as the mallards waddle from the icy river and
            dart

                    and

            dive

                        towards their scraps of bread.
It's as if they've never seen ducks out of water before.

Mother shakes her head at the sight of the bread,
What a waste, she says.

I think of Mr Brown's needy flock of sheep,
        the never-ending
                herding,
                feeding,
                lambing,
                and shearing
(not to mention the rats in his barn).
And I find myself wondering if Mrs Barker is right.

Can they really do their bit here?
And why would they want to, anyway?

But then I think of where they could be instead –
    a factory,
    an office,
    a telephone exchange,
    a hospital –
and what kind of choice is that?

I wonder how many women there are in England
wanting to play their part
and none of them allowed to be heroes.
It just isn't fair.

What a waste,
Mother says again.

Sunday 5ᵗʰ January 1941

And so my role in the war effort begins.
Mother shows me how to nestle
the dull-brown seed potatoes
in egg boxes she has saved,
blunt end up,

eyes gazing skywards.

I think of Ralph
in a crisp blue uniform,
snug in his Spitfire,
soaring through the skies.

It's important, she says,
for the shoots to grow
so that they are ready to plant out
as soon as the conditions are right.
And I think to myself
that however tall I grow,
the conditions will never be right for me to become a hero.

———

What is Mr Fisher doing here?

From over my schoolbook,
I peep across at him

in the chair by the fire,
newspaper unopened on his lap.
He's gazing at the flames
(as he has been all evening),
without saying a word.

It's almost as if the
clacking of Mother's knitting needles
and the flickering flames in the grate
have taken him
somewhere else entirely.

Come to think of it,
I don't know where he spent the whole day.
He can't have gone to Oakmoor and back –
the trains don't run on Sundays
and he doesn't have a motor.

He *does* have a bike
but the ground's still far too icy to use it
and it's been in the shed all day.

No, wherever he's been today,
he's been on foot.
And the question is,
    where?

Because, apart from cows and sheep,
the snow-covered heath
and the fields that are dotted with barns,

the post office, church and village school,
and grumpy Mrs Barker's shop,
    there's nothing for miles around.

He hasn't been helping with the cows.
    I know that for a fact –
        Father was grumbling about doing it all on his own
        at teatime.
He hasn't been with the Home Guard.
    I know that too –
        Mr Brown asked about our new lodger when he
        came to talk to Mother.

And he's certainly not our new warden –
    Revd Collins made it very clear at church this morning
    that he intends to keep on doing that.
And anyway, he's been wearing his RAF uniform
    as if he had a job to do,
        all alone in the hills.

While Mr Fisher continues gazing,
the flames continue flickering and
Mother's needles continue clacking,
I pretend to do my homework and
try desperately to knit it all together.

But no matter how hard I try,
I can't.

Monday 6th January 1941

Has he arrived yet?
    Carol asks in the playground first thing.
        I nod.

What's he doing here?
    Barbara Robinson wants to know.
        I shrug.

Is he nice?
    Nancy Edwards demands.
        I shake my head.

Hang on – what do you mean
you don't know what he does?
    Betty Sanders says,
        and before she gives me a chance to reply,
she's off once again, talking for Britain,
    listing all those reserved occupations I've been through
already.

He's none of those,
    I say, when she finally pauses for breath.
        He's RAF.

Surely that can't be right?
    says Carol.
He'd be over at Oakmoor

if that were the case.
There aren't any planes here.

Perhaps he's an imposter!
 Barbara Robinson says.

With a stolen uniform,
 Nancy Edwards adds.

AND HE'S REALLY A SHIRKER!
 Betty Sanders says, aghast.

And somehow,
before we've even got into the schoolroom,
the whole class thinks there's a slacker lodging in my house
trying to avoid being called up.

Chicken coop, chicken coop!

Bonnie lives in a chicken coop!

the boys chant as they swap their matchbox covers.
I feel my face turning red
and I look at the ground so that they can't see.

What's it like living with a chicken?
little Larry Kendal asks.

I don't say anything.

Cluck, cluck, cluck,

Tommy Jones struts past me,
waggling his elbows
and giggling.

Hey, why don't you give him a white feather?
Nancy Edwards says,
trying to be nice.
To shame the lily-livered coward into doing his duty?

She must have plenty of those in her chicken coop!
John Michael says,
Feathers – get it?
The boys laugh wildly.
And this time some of the girls join in too.

I feel the tears welling up,
but I know I mustn't cry –
that'll make them laugh even more.
And besides, heroes have to be brave.

You know what?
Bonnie's a chicken too!
John Michael says,
clearly noticing my tears.
So her Mr Fisher must feel right at home!

He's not her *Mr Fisher,*
And she's not *a chicken,*

Carol says firmly,
putting her arm through mine and coming to my rescue.
Just as she always does.

By the end of the day,
everyone's joined in the game.
Everyone, that is, except Carol,
who's put them all in their place.
But she has to go back home with Barbara Robinson so
she gives me a hug and says goodbye
and then
    I trudge across the village green
and down the
                slippery
                      lane

all alone.

Tuesday 7th January 1941

I don't like standing   alone   at breaktime and
                watching the others whisper about me.
                I don't like them teasing and taunting and
                seeing them swap their matchbox covers
                                with everyone but me.
                And I don't like the way they're saying that
Mother and Father should never have taken the scrimshanker in
        (although I agree with them one hundred percent).

                At least Carol stands up for me.
                They're simply doing their bit,
                like everyone else, she says.
                And Mr Fisher is too.
                He's got the uniform to prove it.
        And anyway, conchies aren't billeted on dairy farms
                to while the days away.
                Shows how much you all know.
                And with that, she turns away from them,
                links her arm through mine
                and we march off,

VICTORIOUS.

Wednesday 8th January 1941

There's only one thing for it.
I need to find out what Mr Fisher actually does,
get some proof that he's playing his part,
and win my friends back.

> (That's three things – I know.
> But I'll start with the first.)

Saturday 11ᵗʰ January 1941

Early on Saturday
  I creep downstairs,
    avoiding the creaky step,
      placing each foot carefully
        in time with the clock's ticking
          so as not to wake Mother.
          In the kitchen
          I eat my toast and dripping
          and start to write a note for Mother,
    but before I know it, she's there
in the doorway.

Quickly, I shove my satchel
  with its notebook,
  magnifying glass
  and emergency ration of pear drops
under the table,
out of sight.

I can't have Mother knowing what I'm up to.

You're up early, Duck,
she says,
opening a drawer and taking out her gardening gloves.
You've even beaten the men!
Still, just as well
because you've got a busy day ahead.

I can't believe what I'm hearing!
Today was the perfect day for following Mr Fisher,
    for solving the mystery and finding the truth.
It was the day to get the proof I need
    to help me win my friends back.
It was definitely NOT the day for digging the vegetable patch.

═════════

Now that the snow has melted
    and the ground's not as hard,
    it's a perfect opportunity to
    turn the soil over
    and prepare for the spring.

Mother shows me how to use the big heavy spade,
pushing it in with my foot,
tipping soil into the barrow.
She shows me how to work along in a line in front of the
chicken run
until I have dug a trench.
My hands are blistered
and my forehead is covered in sweat.

I stop for a moment and think of Grandfather
digging trenches in the Great War.

Mother shows me how to use manure *to line the trench.*

It improves the soil quality, she says.

And then it's back to digging:
a second trench alongside the first.
But this time, instead of the barrow,
I empty it into the first
until it's all filled in
and no one would ever know
just HOW MUCH time and effort it's taken.
No one, that is, except the chickens
who've been watching by the fence.

I lean on my spade and think of Grandfather
and all the medals he received for his contribution.

And then I start again.

———

Along the lane
and above the clucking of hens,
there comes the sound of singing,
quietly at first,

but louder and louder
until I can hear all the words,

> Join in! Join in!
> There are jobs to be done
> Down in the fields – let us go!
> There's a war to be won,
> And who needs a gun
> When we can be armed with a hoe?

The land girls are smiling
        and laughing
        and swinging their
arms
as they pass the garden gate.
I don't know why they're so happy
and sounding so heroic –
it's not as if digging ditches for Mr Brown is really going to
win the war.

> I've only done a morning of this
> and I'd swap my spade for a gun
>   any day.

Sunday 12th January 1941

Carol comes round in the morning
to ask if I want to knit socks.

I don't.

I hate knitting –
especially socks.
And I doubt there's a soldier out there
who's pleased to receive the ones I've knitted.

But even knitting socks would beat
what I've got to do today.
I take Carol outside to show her what I've dug already.
She's not impressed.
	I can tell.

But I'm mighty glad she's with me
when the boys from school come down the lane.
Tommy Jones is still clucking like a chicken
and laughing like he's just come up with a brand-new joke.
The others don't even try to hide the fact that they're spying –
trying to spot Mr Fisher up to nothing, no doubt.
They don't though.
He's off somewhere –
doing something.

	Although I've absolutely no idea what.

You should be ashamed of yourselves,
     Carol says.
Spying indeed.
Do you know what happens to people who are caught spying?
That shuts them up.
Even Tommy Jones stops clucking.
Perhaps Mr Roberts can tell you.
And with that she strides back towards the house, as if to fetch Father.

And the boys scarper.

━━━━━

                    By the time the evening arrives
I have:
          six trenches dug and filled;
               five days to wait until the weekend;
                    four huge blisters
                         (three of which have burst);
                              two pieces of unfinished homework;
                                   one friend left in the whole world;

          and still

no idea what on earth
Mr Fisher is doing here.

Monday 13th January 1941

Still feeding your chicken?
little Larry Kendal asks,
s ^c a ^t t ^e r ⁱ n ^g a handful of imaginary grain
onto the frosty playground.
Needless to say, that sets Tommy Jones off,
    strutting and squawking
        and pecking and clucking
and soon everyone's flocking round us
        and the flurry of jabbing and jibing,
of shrieking and screeching
          puts me in a right old flap.
        My heart's beating fast,
      like wings thrashing inside my chest
and I scrabble around desperately—

      How many more times?
      Carol explodes,
      He's RAF.

Yeah, yeah, yeah! John Michael replies.
Don't think our mothers haven't seen him
lounging in Bonnie's sitting room all day!
He's a scrimshanking shirker – that's what he is.
And whose side are you on anyway?

Carol's cheeks begin to redden
and her hands start to tremble
as she fights this fight for me.

37

When I get home
at five past four
Mr Fisher's still there
in his chair
by the fire.

Snoring.

The shoes
I polished
so carefully
last night
still where I left them
on the threadbare mat.

Unworn.

I go outside to turn things over.
And as I dig,
questions wriggle to the surface of my mind
like the worms beneath my feet.

Why is he here in the middle of nowhere?

What has he done all day?

Why does he never speak to anyone?

When will he go away?

Tuesday 14th January 1941

I don't need my satchel,
my magnifying glass and
my emergency pear drops
to understand what
muddy shoes that have been kicked off by the door
mean.

Mr Fisher's been out all night.

———

At school today everyone's talking –
Plymouth's been hit overnight
and John Michael's second-cousin-once-removed has lost his
home.
It's not long before they all turn on me –
if shirkers like mine would only do their bit,
none of this would be happening
and children wouldn't be homeless.
Why did you have to take him in? they say.
    As if *I* had a say in it.
    And anyway, he's *not* my shirker.

I turn to Carol.
She'll shut them up –
she always does.

They could be right, you know,
is all she says,
shrugging her shoulders slightly.

I can't believe what I'm hearing.
This isn't supposed to happen.

I mean, Bonnie,
    Carol continues gently,
what does he actually do?
What can *he do out here, in the middle of nowhere?*

    And if he is a shirker –

            well... *they do have a point.*

            ═══════

        I may not get medals for digging,
            or a green and gold shiny badge,
                it won't make me a hero
        and it certainly won't bring my friends back,
            but there's one thing it's good for:

                giving
                me
                time
                to
                think.

41

And Carol's certainly given me lots to think about.

———

So far,
I've dug seven trenches.
(I would've done more
but it gets dark so early.)

And here's what I've uncovered:

The mud on his shoes
tells me that Mr Fisher's
been out every night this week.

I know that he leaves
at half past eight
(that's when I hear the door creak).

He takes his bike
(though goodness knows why –
it must be hard to ride in the blackout).

The heathland heather
caught up in his spokes
tells me exactly where he's been.

The fact that he's snoring
at half past seven

shows he's back before then.

The teeny bits of wire
on the soles of his shoes
are a baffling clue, I confess.

But for a brand-new detective
of just twelve years old
I've done fairly well, nonetheless.

Wednesday 15th January 1941

Carol comes to school clasping a leaflet
and goes round asking everyone if they'd like to join her
    (and Barbara Robinson, of course)
in a search for old rags.

If we collect enough,
we might get awarded a Cog badge,
she says excitedly.

The shiny red-and-white badge in the leaflet looks swell –
I imagine being presented with one,
having it pinned to my chest,
parading up and down at school
and everyone admiring it.
It's probably the closest I'll ever get to being a hero.

But Carol doesn't ask me.

It's fine.
Collecting rags is hardly what I'd call heroic anyway.

Friday 17ᵗʰ January 1941

I've had enough of this:
of being alone at school,
of whispers and sniggers
and being left out,
of not having friends come to call.
And now even Carol's snubbed me,
Carol – my best friend for ever and ever,
who's always stayed by my side,
who's defended me,
fought for me,
taken each blow for me,
and who now,
clearly,
has given up the fight.

I want things back as they used to be.
So I've made a decision
and there's no going back –
tonight is the night
to put it all right.
I'll take my satchel,
magnifying glass and pear drops,
and by the light of the moon
I'll follow Mr Fisher
and discover the truth
once and for all.

Of course,

following Mr Fisher is going to take an awful lot of courage
(and a little bit of rule breaking) –

    I don't think Tommy Jones

    (or even John Michael)

    would dare do this.

Because if Mr Fisher crosses the heath,

    (as I've already worked out that he must)

        he first has to go to the end of the lane,

            past the ramshackle barn,

                and through

                    the field with Father's angry bull.

And although I've never dared do it alone before…

        …tonight it's worth the risk.

Straight after supper I feign a yawn and say goodnight.
Must be all this digging, Father says.
He's right, of course.
Only he has no idea what kind of digging I've been up to.
Tires one out!
And there he's wrong:
I've never
in my whole life
felt more awake.

Mr Fisher glances up from his plate
and looks at me curiously
as if reading my mind.
But before my cheeks have chance to redden,
he nods and returns to his food.

I'd planned to catch some sleep
before setting out.
But now that I'm in bed,

that I can't even close my eyes –

Grandfather serving in the trenches,
   Ralph fighting in the skies,
   Mother and Father keeping the soldiers fed,
   Carol finding rags to make dyes.
   They're all cogs
   in this big war machine
      (even me with my digging, so Mother says).
   But what part does Mr Fisher play?

I'm desperate to find out the truth,
to get all the proof that I need,
to make everything right again.
And I can actually feel the excitement pumping round my
veins
as I think about it.
This must be how Ralph feels all the time.

———

Heart hammering,
adrenalin pumping,
fingers trembling,
   I step
         out
   into the night.

Keep up, keep up,
I tell myself as I walk down the garden path,
anxious not to lose him.

Slow down,
      S   l   o   w   d   o   w   n,
I reply, scared of being caught.
Not that there's any chance of him seeing me out here:
the night's as thick as tar
and I can barely see past my own nose.

I fumble for my bike by the front wall
and check that the lights are hooded –
I can't have him seeing me when they're on,
and having Revd Collins spotting me just doesn't bear thinking
about.

This seemed a good idea in daylight.
But the dynamo won't generate light without speed
and it's far too dark for that.

Still, I need to get some answers
if I want my friends back.

Keep up, keep up,
I tell myself, anxious not to lose him.
      Slow down,
      S   l   o   w   d   o   w   n,
I reply, scared of being caught.

I'm in the saddle,
right foot on the pedal,
and before I know it, I'm off.

I cannot see him up ahead
but I know he's there –
I saw him shut the door behind him
and I know he's heading to the heath.

Keep up, keep up,
I tell myself, anxious not to lose the man I cannot see
(and anxious for the lights to come on).

But suddenly
(before they do)
    Slow down, will you?
a deep voice shouts
as I am tossed from my seat
into a scared and limb-tangled heap.
And when I look up,
I find that I am staring into the stubbly face
of Mr Howard.

Sorry, I mutter,
(for I suppose that even conchies deserve an apology
for being ridden into at full speed,
although I know many who'd disagree).

No harm done,
he says gruffly.
Just take more care next time.

Trust the conchie to spoil everything.
I didn't even make it to the end of the lane.

Eyes smarting,
arm throbbing,
knees wobbling,
I push the bike slowly
back
the
way
I came,
leave it against the wall
and hobble back inside.

Saturday 18th January 1941

You'll have to come up with a different plan.
Mother explains,
Here's the one I drew up last year.

She talks through the diagram
and explains (in great detail)
the principles of crop rotation.
How vegetables shouldn't be planted
in the same place twice.
How they need to be moved on each year:
    potatoes
    then roots
    then brassicas
    then beans…

But I'm not really listening.

    I'm trying to come up with a different plan.

Sunday 19ᵗʰ January 1941

I spin the wheel in my hand,

And I watch the head of the dynamo

But if I want those lights to come on sooner
so that I'm not pedalling in the dark,
it's going to have to go even faster than that.

I think of Ralph on his big bike,
flying off into the distance
            and leaving me behind,
            legs spinning frantically,
            alone in the lane.

Come on, slow coach!
> he used to say.
> And he never would listen
> when I blamed it on my smaller wheels.

Stop making excuses
> is all he'd say.

But I still think I was right, you know –
smaller needs to be faster.
> I'm absolutely sure it does.

So if the head of the dynamo were smaller still—

But that's a completely useless thought.

Because it's not.
And it doesn't help me with my plan.

Monday 20th January 1941

Battery-powered lights are what I need –
I should have seen it before!
They'll come on straight away
and see the end of my problem.

But when I look at the coins in my rusty old tin,
my heart

      sinks

        as I realise
the war will be lost and
Mr Fisher long gone
before I have enough.

And grumpy old Mrs Barker
in the village shop
will never agree to a discount.

There's nothing for it –
I have to ask Carol
but she just turns her head,
Can't help, I'm afraid.

And before I know it,
the whole class is sniggering once again –
asking why on earth I need new-fangled lights.

I make up some story
about helping Father to
round up the cows in the dark.

A few of them seem to buy it.

    For a minute.

But then they just fall about laughing,

Shutting up the chickens more like!

I can't believe that Carol's abandoned me
after all these years together.
I don't think I'll be able to forgive her.

Not ever.

Tuesday 21st January 1941

So I hardly know whether to laugh or cry
when Carol follows me back across the village green and down
the lane and –
    looking over her shoulder as if to check that no one's there –
thrusts me her brother's set of bicycle lamps
(battery-powered, of course).
She smiles at me sadly,
He won't need them while he's away,
so you can use them.

She makes as if to go
    but, with a final glance behind her says,
I'm sorry about everything,
but they were making my life so miserable,
I just couldn't take any more.

As I said, I hardly know whether to laugh or cry –
she deserted me
but without knowing it
she's also come to my rescue.
I can't think what to say,
        so

I
give
her a pear
drop.

I'm so busy trying to work out how I feel,
I almost fail to notice that

shoots

are now growing
from the eyes of the wrinkled potatoes
that gaze upwards.

But I do.

═══════

With the lights on my bike,
the bag in my hand
and one pear drop fewer than last time,
I sneak out and
attempt to win back my friends once more.

And this time I make it to the end of the lane –
and even to the ramshackle barn.

It's not easy with the blackout hood.
Focusing on the ground ahead and
keeping close enough to Mr Fisher

but far enough back not to be seen
     – or, for that matter, heard –
takes all my concentration.
My fingers don't want to unlatch the gate
at the edge of the angry-bull field –
     I'm terrified he'll see me and charge.
     But I haven't got time to get worried and scared –
     if I don't go now, Mr Fisher will be gone.
     So I focus on the darkness,
         how it'll hide me,
           and help me imagine the bull's not there.
     And with a loooooooooooooong

     D

     E

     E

     E

     E

     E

     P

     b r e a t h,
     closed eyes and
     a silent prayer,
somehow, I unlock it,
somehow, I grip back onto the handlebars,
and somehow (to the sound of my own thudding heartbeat),
     I pedal all the way across the endless field.

I don't even see the bull,
but by the time I've got through the far gate

and am out on the heath
I'm utterly e x h a u s t e d.

But I WILL find the answers
and get the proof that I need,
    and I push myself on,

            up the sandy path and

                through the wiry heather
                    until Mr Fisher comes to a **s t o p**
                        thirty yards ahead of me
                            at the crest of the hill.

        I switch off the light and
        lay the bike down,
        keeping it well off the path.
        And that's when I notice
        something most strange –
        the sky here's not so dark,
        as if it's been lit up somehow.

I watch as Mr Fisher's silhouetted form
looks around and lights a cigarette.
Doesn't he know how much trouble he could be in
for attracting the attention of German pilots?
Back in the village, Revd Collins would report him for sure.

But up here on the heath,
well, I suppose there's only him.

And, for that matter, me.

But suddenly there's not only him,
for another dark figure approaches.
And although I can't make out the words,
there's an exchange of deep voices.

I think back to last Friday in the lane
and wonder if it's Mr Howard
he's meeting here in secret.
Perhaps everyone at school is right after all
and I really *am* living with a shirker.

Walking his bike alongside him,
Mr Fisher
and his companion
s l o w l y
make their way
away from me,

over the crest of the hill

and beyond.

Slowly,
I follow,
bent over double,
not
daring
to stand t
          a
          l
          l.
On reaching the top,
I see at once why the sky is lighter –
for stretched out before me
down on the heather
                is a long straight line of lights
leading directly away from our village.

Or,
I realise with horror,
from a German's point of view

(flying in from the south),

directly

TOWARDS OUR VILLAGE.

So that's it!
It's even worse than they think:
he's not a shirker –
he's helping the enemy.
Mr Fisher IS the enemy.

Which makes me wonder if he's Mr Fisher at all,
Perhaps the cold, unsmiling man
who never speaks and
seems somewhere else entirely
is not a Mr Fisher,
but a

Herr Fischer.

Heart t^{h}u^{d}d^{i}n^g
like gunfire,
feet p^{o}u^{n}d^{i}n^g the heath,
I race bullet-fast to my bike.
Wheels whizz through wiry heather,
charge past the angry bull
        (who no longer even seems a threat)
and
shoot
        up the lane.

Once back in my room,
I suck furiously on a pear drop.

If this isn't an emergency,
I don't know what is.

The idea that we might be living with a chicken
filled me with shame,
    embarrassment,
anger,
            and resentment.

But living with a German spy
    quite
    simply
    fills
    me
    with
    absolute
    TERROR.

═══

Long after I get back,
my heart is still p o u n d i n g
just as fast as it was.
New images and fears flash through my mind
like bullets from a machine gun
or seeds sprinkled on the soil:

my village bombed,

invaded,

attacked;

buildings raided,

looted

ransacked;

prisoners taken,

tortured

and—

None of them have time to take root and grow into proper
ideas.

Until
my heartbeat finally
            begins
            to s l o w,
my breathing calms,
and I can think clearly again.
I realise that
        the news I'm living with a spy
            is the last thing I need spread at school,
                but…
                    if I play my cards right,
                        I could
                        (just maybe,
                    perhaps)
            save the village
which would,
        (without doubt,
            female or not)
                make

                        me

                    a
            hero
and everyone will simply have to be kind to me then.

The question is,

        how to play my cards right?

I think so hard,
and for such a long time that
I eventually sink into sleep.
And when I do, my dreams are all

mixed up

and things keep changing:
potatoes to roots,
          Ralph to hero,
roots to brassicas,
          Carol to deserter,
brassicas to beans,
          deserter to saviour,
beans back to potatoes
          and Mr Fisher to German spy.

But even though everything's moving,

changing,

rotating,

I'm still not a hero.

Yet.

Wednesday 22nd January 1941

Mother cannot get me up in the morning,
says I'm dead to the world.

I don't think she realises that soon
we may **all** be –

If Herr Fischer isn't stopped.

Which starts my brain racing all over again:
how to stop him,
who to tell,
and how to explain what I've learned.

Certainly not Carol, nor Barbara Robinson, nor Nancy
Edwards,
and heaven forbid Betty Sanders should know!

Blurting it out in a hurry
might put the whole village at risk –
if Mr Fisher finds out, that is.

The Home Guard is the obvious choice
since they're on the lookout for Germans,
        but Mr Brown would tell Mother,
        who'd insist on knowing
        just where I'd been and when.

And I'd be in so much trouble
it just wouldn't be worth it.
No, I need to consider this carefully,
act cautiously, gather the facts.

———

Mother, I'm going to Carol's for lunch today,
I say as c a s u a l l y as I can
whilst I watch her wash the breakfast dishes,
face lit by the morning sun.
She doesn't know that Carol's deserted me.

Is that all right with her family?
Mother asks,
It's fine,
I say.
Well, you'd better take them some eggs from the henhouse.

I scurry to get them,
glad of an excuse to leave the room.
I don't like keeping Mother in the dark.

But sometimes
needs must.

———

As soon as the lunch bell rings
I thrust half a dozen eggs into Carol's hands
          (quickly before anyone can see).
For your mother,

I say, to answer the huge question

that shows on her face.
I don't wait for her to answer
but dash to my bike
propped up against the playground wall.

And, in no time,
I'm flying through the village,
down the lane,
past the ramshackle barn,
across the angry-bull field,
onto the heath,
along the sandy path
and up to the crest of the hill.

I'm really not sure
what I expect to see –
I just want to see it clearly
before I report the man.
Just want to see,
with my own two eyes,
in the very cold light of day.

But whatever I think I know and have seen,
nothing
prepares me

for **THIS.**

Barbed wire.

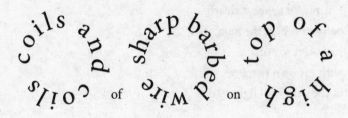

wire fence,
surrounded this side with p r i c k l y g o r s e,
blocking my path

to everything that lies beyond.
There's a gate in the fence,
but it's chained and padlocked
and as far as I look
to the left
and the right,
I can't see any other way in.

Beyond the fence,
like giant picnic rugs
spread out on the heather,
huge sheets of canvas
lie dotted about.

And around them,
not a single person,
but more lorries and cars and trucks than
I've ever set eyes on before.
Not blue and shiny and clean
like the motor Dr Bovingdon sometimes drives,
but green and dusty –
rusty even –
with huge great wheels
and really high cabs.
I wonder if this is how Nancy Edwards felt
when she first saw a field of cows.

But I bet she wasn't half as surprised,
dazed, amazed or confused
as I am when I spot
the ten
ACTUAL SPITFIRES
lined up
on OUR heath.

Not Messerschmitts,
but good solid
English
Spitfires.

And I bet she wasn't half as

delighted

as I am when I realise I've found
a new RAF base
so close to home.

But an RAF base that
(for some reason)

is completely deserted.

I cycle back to school as fast as I can
dying to tell them the news.
No one will believe their eyes when they see this place
but they'll certainly see that Mr Fisher's no scrimshanking shirker.

And then I'll have friends again.

Of course,
I won't get to be the hero that I hoped I'd be
by reporting that he was a spy.
But secretly I'm quite relieved this time –
      finding a way to tell Mr Brown
      without Mother finding out
      might have been just a little

                    tiny bit tricky.

Perhaps I'm just not brave enough to be a hero after all.

But at least I've seen that it's possible
for the conditions to be right
for a girl like me
to be one.

———

I race through the village and across the green,
my heart p o u n d i n g with excitement.
I want to shout out the news from here
so that all the games of hopscotch and skipping and marbles
will suddenly come to a **stop**

and everyone will gather at the playground wall

        asking questions
        and listening
        and wanting to be my friend
        before I've even put my bike away.

But the sight of John Michael suddenly swooping an imaginary
Spitfire round the yard,
and taking everyone by surprise
makes me   **stop**   in my tracks and hold fire.
Perhaps there's a reason no one knows about the airbase,
perhaps it needs to stay that way,
and perhaps, as much as I want my friends back,
I'd better not say anything after all.
Careless talk costs lives, as we all know.

And anyway,
        nobody even looks at me as I enter the playground.

———

Turning over the soil in
my fourteenth trench,
I see things I've not noticed before:
        a stray potato left behind from last year's crop,
                a tightly-coiled creamy-white grub,
        a broken piece of pottery.

And as I toss out the dandelion roots
that have clung so tight in the soil,
I look at things from a different angle:

Mr Fisher's NOT the enemy.
He IS a cog in this wheel of war,
and he MUST be doing some good.

But however much I turn things over,
an explanation for his nightly visits
and the empty air base just
won't come
to the surface.

Saturday 25th January 1941

All week
      (when I'm not at school,
      and Carol,
           no doubt,
      is out and about collecting rags)
I've been digging,
and thinking
and digging.
And although the vegetable patch
      is getting cleared,
nothing is clearer in my head.

And suddenly I hit upon something,
something   h
              a
              r
              d:
perhaps the answer doesn't lie out here.
The stones and the weeds
and the cold on my cheeks
won't give me the answers
I'm looking for.

Instead they're inside,
inside with Mr Fisher.
Cold,
stony-faced,

distant Mr Fisher
who can't be asked any questions.

I grit my teeth and force a smile.
Good afternoon, Mr Fisher,
I say as I enter the room.

                              Good afternoon,
                    he says, barely raising his head
                    from the paper he's absorbed in.

Anything good happened recently?
I ask
(I don't think that counts as a question).

He lowers his paper
and looks at me,

eyebrows   raised

just a fraction towards
his hairline.

                              Nodding slowly
                    (and without a trace of a German accent),
                              he replies:
          Twenty-five thousand Macaroni taken prisoner.

Oh! I say. *Where?*
(that can't be a question either).

Tobruk – it's a port in Libya,
he says,
lifting his paper again,
clearly finished with me.

But I haven't finished with him.
Is that on the Egyptian side?
Or the Tunisian side?
Or somewhere in between?
(That's another three questions, I know,
but I can't believe they count either).

Mr Fisher might think so though,
I worry,
as he folds his paper and
gives me a long hard stare that I don't understand.

You like geography?
he says at last.
(Now that IS a question
because I don't quite know how to answer.)

Yes, I reply finally,
lifting my chin,
still wondering whether to tell him
that I came top of the school
in the test before Christmas
(a whole seven marks higher than Carol).
But I know Mother would tell me not to show off

so instead I take the easy option and say,
Do you?
(surely not really a question either).

> *Hated it.*
> *Always preferred physics myself.*

Physics?
What's that?
(I've absolutely no idea,
so I simply have to ask the question.)

> *Physics,*
> Mr Fisher says
> (with a spark in his eyes
> that I've not seen before),
> *provides the answers to all our questions.*

I like physics already.

Sunday 26th January 1941

Sprinkling the tiny round cress seeds
onto the newspaper (dampened of course)
that Father and Mr Fisher have finished with
doesn't take long, and
is a whole lot easier than digging
the vegetable patch.

And while I do it,
Mr Fisher starts to explain
about tiny things called
atoms.

Wednesday 29th January 1941

Before I know it,
the seeds take root and

tiny

stems

start

to

unfurl

pushing upwards towards the light.

Sunday 2nd February 1941

When the stems
are tall enough to cut,
Mr Fisher explains why they fall

when I make each snip.

Gravity, he calls it.
I ask him to explain
and he tells me that there are lots of different forces,
all working in different ways.

And after our egg and cress sandwiches,
Mr Fisher says he can show me if we take out our bikes.
As we fly down the lane and round the bends
I begin to get a grip on

acceleration

and d   r   a   g

and *centripetal force*

and Mr Fisher's beginning to

smile.

Mother's certainly not though
and gives me an earful when I get back.

What did I tell you about bothering Mr Fisher?
He's a hard-working man
with a crucial job to do,
and he certainly deserves some peace and quiet
of a Sunday afternoon.
And what's more—

It's fine, Mrs Roberts,
comes a voice from the doorway.
I enjoyed it.

That shuts her up.

Monday 3rd February 1941

We saw you!
        Barbara Robinson says,
Flying around with that chicken,
like there's nothing better for him to do.

You should have given him that white feather
back when I told you to,
        Nancy Edwards adds,
        not so nicely this time.
He needs to know that it's not all right
to be dodging his duty
and gallivanting about
while others are dying.
But you're just encouraging him now.

        And I simply have no idea how to reply to that.

        So I say nothing at all.

Tuesday 4th February 1941

Remembering that shiny red-and-white badge
and how it'd make me feel to be seen wearing it at school,
I ask Mother if I can start a collection of my own.
She digs out a ragged old duster;
the torn cushion cover made from Grandmother's wedding dress;
and a pair of Father's socks that have been darned too many times.

I pull out last year's dress (patched and three inches too short)
and stuff it all in the chest under Grandfather's old zoetrope.
And wonder whether I'll ever get enough.

Thursday 6th February 1941

Mother says that
now the digging is done,
it would be wise to hunt for snails.

Before they can do any damage,
she says, when I ask her why.

So,
while Ralph is flying over foreign fields
looking for Germans to kill,

                  I'm searching upturned flowerpots

                                for snails.

Sitting proud and tall behind a huge wheel,
one of the land girls drives down the lane.
I put down my flowerpot
and stop to watch.
It's not an army lorry she's driving –
it's only Mr Brown's tractor,
but she looks happy enough about it.

Father said they were using gas cylinders yesterday
to stop the pests from doing Hitler's work.
I know he was only talking about killing the rats in the hedgerows,
        but even so,
        it beats picking up snails
        one by one with my fingers.

It seems that Mrs Barker was wrong then.

They're still here –

      the land girls that is

            (and probably the rats are too – until the gas gets them).

And they've certainly got more to sing about than me.

Friday 7th February 1941

When Carol (the Eager Beaver)
stands up in front of the class and sings her song
about dustbins and victory,
she tells us all just how well she and
Barbara Robinson are doing with their rags,
and how close they must be to earning A BADGE.

She tells us that what she collects
is not just used for dyes,
but for uniforms,
five-pound notes,
charts and maps,
blankets, rugs,
mattress stuffing,
and the roofs of army huts.

I try to make myself as small as I can
in the back row of the class,
and pray that Miss Price won't ask about my contribution.
        I simply can't admit
        what I'm collecting.

Saturday 8th February 1941

What we've all been waiting for
arrives while Mother and Father
are out with the cows.
I think they'd want me to
save it for them,   so I prop it up on the mantelpiece
                                            next to his photograph
                                                      and wait.

All morning I wait,
and in my head
I see the dogfights,
the bombing raids,
and the smile of victory
on my brother's face.

Mother can't stop beaming when she reads it
and clasps it to her chest.
Father puts an arm around her and smiles.
But Mr Fisher's faraway look comes back;
                              he gazes into the fire
                              and doesn't hear Mother
                              when she says lunch is ready.

But something in Mr Fisher
really lights up when
        (after we've cleared away the dishes
        and Father switches on the floor lamp)
I ask him to explain

how the lamp works.

And when he says he'll teach me
to make an electric circuit tomorrow,
something inside me

lights up
too.

But isn't electricity dangerous?
    I ask.

Only if you don't know what you're doing,
    he replies.
And that's why it's good to learn.

━━━━━

When the grown-ups get their newspapers out
I ask to be excused
and rush to get my bike from the shed.
Opening that letter from Ralph
has made me itch for the world he's now part of
– the planes, the heroes, the glory –
and now that Mr Fisher has opened up another world
– of circuits and forces and gravity –
I simply cannot resist sneaking up to the heath
to look longingly at those lonely Spitfires
from the crest of the hill.

Sunday 9th February 1941

Like whizzing electrons,
there's a fizz of excitement
in my tummy
when I wake up,
and I can hardly wait
until Mr Fisher comes down
so he can show me that circuit.

Bother his overnight outings that keep him in bed so late!

But it doesn't take long for Mother
to find me something to do –
she sends me outside
armed
with a rake,
a trowel
and a packet of spinach seeds.
It's hardly electrifying
and I know what I'd rather be doing.
But at least it beats hunting for snails.

———

Well, I'll be blowed!
If Mr Fisher hasn't got
Carol's bicycle lights
on the kitchen table!

I feel my cheeks start to redden
and my heart beats in my throat –
he must have found me out!

But when he sees me,
Mr Fisher tells me they're his
and is soon so busy

                taking them apart
    and telling me how they work
that he doesn't notice my cheeks.
    And I think I'm safe.

So I start to listen.

And Mr Fisher makes it all so simple.

He explains the necessary components:

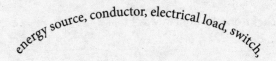

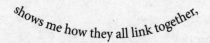

and suddenly a light comes on.
This is so much more interesting than **anything** else I've **ever**
done
and I want to carry on –
 doing more,
   knowing more,
     understanding more,
until everything makes perfect sense.

That doesn't stop me from wanting to be a hero though
 (that's still my NUMBER ONE AIM).

I just wish that heroes used physics.

Sunday 16th February 1941

Mr Fisher watches from the doorway as I make

holes

with the dibber
ready for planting beans
just as Mother's diagram shows.

You're doing a splendid job out here,
he says.
I look around at the bare earth
    free from sticks
    and stones
    and weeds
    and snails;
not a sign of life at all.

It's just an empty nothingness,
bleak and dull and lacking.

Like my role in this war.

But Mr Fisher nods his head.

Just wait.
You'll see.
Very soon.

Monday 17ᵗʰ February 1941

And sure enough,
when I get home from school
t h r e e r o w s o f t i n y g r e e n l e a v e s,
pointed and paired,
have pushed their way up
to the surface.

And before I even have time to think,
I'm calling for Mr Fisher.

Mr Fisher says it's grand
and pats me on the back.
And in celebration of my first victory,
he says he has a surprise for me.

I'm more pleased about the spinach
than I thought I'd be,
but it's hardly a victory.
Not in the Ralph kind of way.
But I do like surprises,
so I keep quiet.

It turns out that Mr Fisher
has an old wireless for me.
It's not the one we have at home

and I've no idea where he's got it from.
But he says we can take it apart
to see the electrics inside.

And as we take off the outer casing
revealing valves and transformers,
capacitors and resistors,

Mr Fisher explains what each part does,

smiles

and even begins to laugh.

It has to be said,
I'm starting to like Mr Fisher.

So I offer him a pear drop.

Tuesday 18th February 1941

The spinach is taller than it was yesterday,
taller and stronger, its leaves longer.

And I find that planting shallots
isn't quite so much of a chore.

Wednesday 19th February 1941

But when I return from school
to find the shallots

strewn
          carelessly   across the
                            soil,

I am utterly
browned
off.

Not just with the pesky blackbirds,
but with the WHOLE digging for victory thing.

Mr Fisher finds me
slumped by the shed,
head in my hands,
satchel on the ground.

They're a blooming nuisance, aren't they?
he says, crouching down beside me,
But I suppose they need to eat too.
Maybe a scarecrow would work?

And I just can't help myself.
        It's not fair!
        I shout,

Every day,

Ralph gets to go off in his Spitfire

and fire at a real live enemy,

and all I ever do is

search for snails and

scare the blackbirds!

Mr Fisher slowly shakes his head.
Trust me, he says,
in that annoying
I'm-a-grown-up-and-I-know-better-than-you way,
You're better off with snails and blackbirds.

And he gets up
and starts replanting
the shallots.

Thursday 20ᵗʰ February 1941

He just doesn't get it.
Doesn't get it at all.
How can I possibly be better off here
in a muddy old garden?
And how dare he tell me that!

I stamp the soil down
    HARD
and decide not to speak to him.

Friday 21st February 1941

Something's been at my spinach overnight.
One-and-a-half rows gone –
just like that.

    How.
    Dare.
    They.

Saturday 22nd February 1941

I heard on the wireless
that Swansea has been almost
completely obliterated.

And Mother's telling me yet again
to search for snails
before they start to nibble at the spinach.
What's left of it.

———

By lunchtime I've had enough
and as soon as I've helped clear up,
I'm off, up to the heath
where I can be away from everything
and just be alone.

And this time,
as I gaze at the Spitfires from the crest of the hill,
I'm imagining all the valves and transformers,
    capacitors and resistors
that I'd find in the cockpits
if only
    I could get past that barbed wire fence,

which I can't.

Sunday 23rd February 1941

Mr Fisher asks me if I want to
make my very own circuit this afternoon.
I really, really,

               really do
but I say, *no*
and then add, *thank you*
when Mother turns her head.
I'm not talking to him, you remember.
And anyway, I'm making a scarecrow.

I go and gather the bits I'll need:
      an old potato sack,
      two long sticks,
      some twine from the shed,
      last year's dress from the chest
      and an armful of straw.

There's an icy wind outside
and I long to be back in the house
but I grit my teeth
and carry on

until my scarecrow stands
tall, its floral dress flapping
relentlessly
around its useless straw-stuffed body.

It needs something else,
I think.
And as I close the clasps
on Grandfather's wooden trunk,
I wonder whether he would approve.

But the scarecrow just looks SO much better
in a trench cap.

Tuesday 25th February 1941

That's a jolly fine scarecrow,
Mr Fisher remarks.
Looks quite heroic out there
in all that weather.
Has it done the trick?

Yes, I have to admit.
And *Thank you,* I add.

So do you fancy making that circuit now?
Mr Fisher continues.
And even though I'm not talking to him,
I find myself n o d d i n g.
And before I know it,
I am cutting up wires,
    melting solder,
        and switching on the lights
    of my very first circuit.

And suddenly,
the day doesn't seem
quite as miserable.

And I am talking to Mr Fisher again.

Thursday 27ᵗʰ February 1941

Mother

blows her fuse

when the Hoover stops working
just an hour before her knitting party
are due to arrive.
Let me have a look, Mrs Roberts,
Mr Fisher says.
He points at the burn mark on the cable,
explains how the wires are damaged inside,
how it's caused a short circuit
with earth now touching live,
and how that's what's blown the fuse.

> Down in the cellar,
> he shows me how
> to snip some wire
> to mend it,
> then upstairs
> together
> we cut the cable,
> take apart the plug
> and wire it up again
> as good as new.

Mother is

delighted.

And, when the knitting party arrive,
everything is shipshape and Bristol fashion
and they can darn evacuees' socks,
knit soldiers' comforters
and patch their own frocks
to their hearts' content.

Friday 28ᵗʰ February 1941

Bobbie
    (that's our scarecrow –
    we've named her)
is doing a splendid job, and
Mr Fisher says that the vegetable patch
is looking tickety-boo.

Broad beans are beginning to
poke
    their
        cautious way
    through the soil, and
new round wrinkled leaves have formed
on the spinach seedlings.
I peep into the top of the rhubarb pots
at stems that are pale, pink and long,
and my mouth waters at the thought
of good things to eat.

Saturday 8ᵗʰ March 1941

And it isn't long
before good things come our way
(in the form of rhubarb crumble
and our own thick cream).

Everyone licks their lips.
We even have seconds today.

Mother, Father and Mr Fisher are full of praise
and, although it doesn't quite make me a hero,
or bring my friends back,
I do feel happy.

═══════

Before we even wipe our mouths
and sit back in our chairs,
there's a clattering at the front door,
urgent and loud.
Father goes to answer it
and all goes quiet.

Until,
at last,
I hear him say,
 No reply,
and Mother puts a hand to her mouth.
I turn to Mr Fisher but he
just shakes his head.

When Father comes back,
he's clutching the telegram,
his face as white as the paper but
his expression as **dark**
as the words written on it:
 `Priority`
it says.

  `Regret to inform you`
  `Pilot Officer Ralph Roberts`
  `reported missing in action March 7`[th]

   ━━━━

Ralph,
you remember how you got upset
when you couldn't stay hidden
in our games of hide and seek?

Well, now you've gone
            and got yourself lost,
            and I'm the one upset.

Ralph,
you remember that you taught me how to spot
a Messerschmitt in the sky above me
(to keep me safe, you said)?

Well, now you've gone
            and who knows if you're safe –
            did you fail to spot one?

Ralph,
you remember that you stole the heart of
every girl in the village (except Mary Smith's,
which I'll never understand)?

Well, now you've gone
            and have been stolen from me
            and have completely broken mine.

Ralph,
you remember how you used to be scared of the dark

and when I was cross with you,
I'd turn out the light?

Well, now you've gone
        and left me in the dark,
        and I've simply no idea
        if the light will ever come back on.

Ralph,
I'm sorry.
Please come back
from wherever
        you've gone.

That is what I want to write
to Ralph.

But I can't
because Ralph is `missing in action.`

So instead,
I ride up to the heath and
        in the gathering gloom
look down at the lonely Spitfires
from the crest of the hill.
And I wish more than anything that
        there were a few wires I could snip,
        some solder I could melt,
        a fuse I could fix
to save my brother from

                    `missing in action`

and turn the light back on inside.

Sunday 9th March 1941

When Mary Smith comes round
to offer her condolences,
and wipes a tear from her eye,
I don't understand.

```
Missing in action
```
seems to
change everything.

> Only Bobbie remains unchanged,
> her dress flap-flapping
> in the breeze,
> the straw-stuffed body
> stands tall
> and strong,
> while mine is empty, numb.

Last summer I wore that dress –
　　　　last summer when Ralph was here.
I tore it when I climbed too high
and it caught in boughs of Mr Brown's tree.
But Ralph (the hero)
helped me down again
and Mother patched it.

I stained it when I slipped in a race
I was running on the green.

But Ralph (still the hero)
helped me up again
and Mother washed it.

I outgrew it when I shot up
before Christmas
and Ralph (ever the hero)
went off to fight.

And now there's nothing Mother can EVER do
to make it right again.

I wonder about the trench cap.
I thought it'd make Bobbie
look more heroic.
But it's

soggy

and it's

slipped down over her face.
And a pigeon has left
its mark.

And for the first time,
I realise that Ralph
was a hero to me
long before he became
        missing in action.

Mr Fisher sits down beside me
on the cold wooden bench.

I've never met your brother Ralph,
he says,
but I know that he means a lot.
And I also know
that not knowing
is hard.
And I just wanted to say—

But he doesn't get to finish
because I cut him off.
You don't know anything!
I shout.
And I leave him sitting there with Bobbie,
her dress flap-flapping
in the breeze.

Monday 10th March 1941

All the grown-ups in the village try to make me feel better:
    Revd Collins says that his cousin
    was reported missing in action at Ypres,
    but that he turned up
    in a hospital five weeks later.

    Miss Price's uncle
    turned out to be a prisoner of war
    after thirteen months of no word.

    And Mrs Barker's nephew
    was even reported `killed in action,`
    but turned up as right as rain.
    Mistaken identity, she said.

But Ralph isn't Revd Collin's cousin,
nor is he Miss Price's uncle,
and he certainly isn't grumpy Mrs Barker's nephew.
    He's my brother.
    And he's only nineteen years old.

———

Oh, and another thing that hasn't changed
is the teasing and taunting at school.
Bonnie the Hen-Keeper is what they're calling me now
or *the Chicken Crony*
or *the Scrimshanker's Sidekick*.

Carol gives me a sad look
and for a moment I think she'll apologise
and be my friend again.
But then she turns away fast.

   I can never forgive her for this.

—————

How about doing some more electrics?
Mr Fisher asks when I get home.

But electrics won't fix anything.
And I tell him so.

Tuesday 11ᵗʰ March 1941

Today I get home to find Mr Fisher,
shirt sleeves rolled up,
raking the soil in the vegetable patch.
Thought I'd help you prepare your seed beds,
he says.
It's a fine day and the soil's not too wet.

     I stand and watch.
I know I shouldn't,
but I do.
The thing is,
I just don't seem able to do ANYTHING.
Not with Ralph `missing in action`.

But Mr Fisher doesn't seem to mind.
Pass me the parsnip seeds,
he says when he's finished.
And I do.
     And then I stand and watch
while he sows them in clusters
six inches apart.

We'll thin them later.
Now for the lettuces,
he says, holding out his hand.
And I pass him the packet.
     And stand and watch.

We'll just plant one row for now –
we'll do another in two weeks' time.
That way we'll get a constant supply.

Leeks next,
he says.
Now radishes,

and parsley

and peas.

And all the time,
     I stand and watch.

I know I shouldn't,
but I do.

Wednesday 12th March 1941

When he's planted the brussels sprouts,
Mr Fisher asks for the reel of black cotton.
To keep the birds off, he says.
Bobbie's a bit far from here.
He winds it round a twig in the ground
and passes it back to me.
In turn, I wind the reel and pass;
he winds and passes back.
We continue like this for a good half hour:
back and forth,
back and forth
until the row is covered,

and I've done something.

We sit on the old wooden bench
and look at the seedbeds we've sown.

They look so bare and empty now,
says Mr Fisher,
and it's hard to imagine
they'll ever thrive.

But mark my words,
they will.

Friday 14th March 1941

Mother tells me to
take the tin watering can
and give everything a good sprinkling
as it's been
   so dry
the last few days.

                  L
                  i
                  k
                  e
               tears,
         the droplets
            fall onto

   the finely-raked earth.

I try to imagine the tiny seeds stirring below the surface,
desperate to find their way through the dark,
into the sun.

I wipe my cheek with the back of my hand
and wonder if Ralph will ever come home.

Saturday 15th March 1941

Here again.
But this time, as I turn to go from the crest of the hill,
and back through the wiry heather,
I realise I haven't been thinking my usual thoughts.
Not once have I thought about heroes and glory,
about circuits and forces and wires.

I glance back over my shoulder
at the closest Spitfire.

Please just bring him home.

Sunday 16th March 1941

When I carry the watering can
across to the seed beds this morning,

there are two perfectly straight

rows of tiny green specks.

I rush over and bend down to
have a closer look, and
see pairs of tiny heart-shaped leaves
joined at each stem,
smaller, but like the clover
I used to search through
on the village green.

I never found a four-leaf one,
but Ralph did,
        once.

He told me it'd bring him luck.

I hope he was right.

Friday 16ᵗʰ May 1941

By the time it's Ralph's birthday though,
I'm beginning to seriously doubt it.
There's been no word
and he's still `missing in action`.
How can someone just disappear like that?

Mary Smith has come round to offer more best wishes
        (why would she even know it's his birthday?)
and Mother invites her in for tea.
We light a candle on the cake she's made
and start to sing the usual song.
But one by one our voices crack
and silence takes over.

Even Mr Fisher brushes away a tear.

No one can bring themselves
to blow out the candle
when we reach the final word in our heads.

So instead,
we watch it
burn
slowly
all the way
to the bottom,
where it
f l i c k e r s
weakly
and dies.

Saturday 17th May 1941

But I mustn't give up on Ralph.
I can't.
        I won't.
He must be out there somewhere.
        I simply know he must.

And all of a sudden,
I long to be close to him,
to feel part of his world
and to understand everything that he must have been through.

That's when I make a decision –
there IS a way I can feel closer to Ralph.
I've known it before,
but never quite dared to do it
        for fear of getting hurt.
But the scratches on my skin will be nothing
compared to the pain I already feel inside.

So I check that Mr Fisher's still safely in bed,
        tell Mother that I'll be back for lunch
                and, before she has chance to ask me more,
                        I've grabbed my bicycle
                        and am heading down the lane,
                        through the angry-bull field,
                        and up the sandy path
                        through the heather.

It's only nine but already warm,
and I don't know
whether it's that
           or the anticipation
that's making me sweat.

I can't get through the wire fence,
 but if I follow it round the outside edge
       through all that prickly gorse,
I'll be able to get closer to the planes.
   And however long it takes me,
    however scratched I might get,
standing right beside an actual Spitfire
        will bring me closer –
           much closer –
             to Ralph,
        than I've ever been before.

So leaving my bike by the gate,
I trample my way through the bright-yellow gorse,
stamping down the long green needles,
and crushing the flowers beneath my feet.
I clutch tightly to the wire fence
to keep my balance
         as I ^{tiptoe} my way
                 around
             the larger shrubs.

130

Shins scratched and bleeding,
        hardly caring,
            heart racing,
I keep my eyes firmly on my feet,
willing them on –
            longing to know
                    and be part of
                            Ralph's world.

And when
        at last
I think I must be closer,
        I raise my head –

AND STOP

DEAD,

not believing my eyes.

            And not wanting to believe them.

For there, lined up on the other side of the fence –

                    no painted metal,
                    no smooth propeller,
                    no sunken rivets,
                    no circuits in the cockpit.

Just ten hollow wooden frames,
each draped in thin canvas
and propped up on wooden stilts.
Not real Spitfires at all.

No more real than Bobbie
with her straw-stuffed body
and flapping dress,
and as utterly useless to anyone
as a searcher of blackbirds and snails.

Why are they here?
What is the point?
Why fill our heath
(in the middle of nowhere)
with useless fakes?

And what on earth does Mr Fisher do here,
night after night

            after night?
I thought he had a job to do,
thought he was playing his part,
thought he deserved to wear that officer's uniform?

But it's clearly all a game to him,
just a great pretence,
which means that
he's as much a fraud

as everyone says,
as the airplanes lined up before me,
and the straw-stuffed scarecrow
        he told me to make.

And that makes me MAD.

———

Once again,
        I'm back on my bike,
        speeding across the heath.
Fuelled by fury,
        I pick up a whole new
        kind of momentum.
Heart hammering,
        hot and
        ready to burst,
                I'm the angry bull in the field today.
        I race past the ramshackle barn
        and speed up the lane.
I'll go straight to his room,
        hammer the door down,
        wake him up,
                I don't care.
                (It's not his room anyway –
                it's Ralph's.)
Ralph who's done

something useful,
                put himself in danger
            and has been `missing in action`
                    for *sixty-one* whole days.

Mr Fisher

                    does NOT

            deserve

to be in there.

But when I get home,
out of breath
and furious,
I see that he's not.

He's out watering my vegetables.

                                Good morning, Bonnie.
                                        I thought I'd –
                                    he starts to say,
                        Oh! Is everything all right?

No, it's absolutely not,
~~I shout.~~
You should be ashamed of yourself,
for not going to fight in the war,
*you're a **coward** and a **shirker***

and
how can you live with yourself,
doing nothing each night
while boys like my brother
*risk their **lives every***
> ***single***
>> ***day?***

The watering can dangles
from Mr Fisher's hand,
his face quite blank,
expressionless,
and – if he were wearing a flowery dress –
I'd say he looked like Bobbie.

> > > *What?*
> > is all he says.

And for a dreadful moment
I think I've got it all wrong.
But how can he
not
know
what I'm talking about?

Mr Fisher sits down heavily
on the old wooden bench and
somehow he looks older
than he's done before.

He rests his elbows on his knees,
his chin in his hands
and with his head he motions me
to sit beside him.

I hardly know what to do –
I don't want to obey
        but
my anger's lost some of its fire
now that I've let it out.
And Mr Fisher seems
almost sad, somehow.

So I stand beside him,
head hung low
and wait
        awkwardly for him to speak.

               What makes you think this?
                  is all he says
                     finally.

And I mutter something about fake planes
in deserted heathland where nothing's going on.

Mr Fisher shuts his eyes
and nods his head,
chin still in his hands
        for what seems like forever.

Bonnie, you're to stay away from there,
he says at last.
You understand?

So he doesn't want me spying on him –
doesn't want me to know just how little he does!
Too late – I already do.
My fists clench tightly,
my heart beats fast
and my face feels hot,
but before I explode again,
he's changed the subject
and something in his voice makes me listen.

Tell me what you see over there,
he says,
nodding towards the potato plants.

Potatoes?
I answer through gritted teeth.

*But tell me
EXACTLY what you see,*
he says.

*Green leaves,
stems,*
I answer slowly,
unsure where this is going.

Useful to us?
he asks.

No.

Any sign of potatoes?
Actual potatoes, I mean.

No.

And why not?

I pause
and then say,
Why, they're hidden below the surface,
of course.

Indeed.
Mr Fisher replies.
And he gets up and walks inside.

Now it's my turn
to stand in confusion
probably looking even more like Bobbie
than Mr Fisher did
(on account of my dress).

So, I've failed to see

the true value of what
he does?

And did he mean that
like the potatoes
beneath the soil
he's going to do us some good?
Keep us alive, perhaps?

Somehow, I think that's unlikely
for however hard
I picture those planes –
empty canvas shells on stilts –
I have no idea what they're for.

Mr Fisher told me to build a scarecrow
to frighten away the blackbirds.
But surely ten fake stationary Spitfires
aren't going to scare off the Germans?

And I can't think what else they'd be for.

I don't know how long
I stand like that,
dress flapping gently in the breeze,
but I'm so full of questions,
and what's more,
I'm beginning to feel an aching guilt
for shouting at Mr Fisher.

He's been so kind in other ways –
planting my seeds,
teaching me physics,
and being almost like

                              a friend.

I've wanted to trust him,
to believe he's playing his part
even if I can't see it.
And I really don't want the taunts to be true –
I don't want to be Bonnie the Hen-Keeper,
a mere coward's friend.
I can be more than this,

I know I can.

So if there IS a reason
for all the mysterious things he does,
I need to see it
with my very own eyes.

And so I decide
that's exactly what I'm going to do.
I'll watch Mr Fisher
up on the heath,
see what he ACTUALLY does,
and then I'll know,
once and for all,
if he's really doing something good.

And I'll do it
    this very night.

———

I don't need to follow
Mr Fisher this time.
I know where I'm going
and don't want to be caught.
So, when I hear him leave at half past eight
I wait
    for what
        seems like
            forever,
before slipping out unseen.
I'm right out of pear drops,
so I pull up a couple of radishes,
    wipe off the soil
and throw them in my satchel,
    just in case.

The evening is warm,
the air is still,
and even though it's ten o'clock,
the sun still hangs low in the sky.
The heath stretches out in front of me and everything's so
peaceful,
it seems hard to imagine
that I could ever need the gas mask

     slung over my shoulder in its cardboard box
or that there is a war on at all.

And as I pedal,
I begin to hear
a strange mechanical sound.
I stop,
I wonder,
and cock my head
listening more carefully
to the churring call

      rises
that   and
          falls.

And that's when I see it,

twisting and turning silently
as it glides across the heath:
    a nightjar.

——————

The sun is close to setting
as I reach the crest of the hill.
I check the gate but it's still locked,
so I leave my bike
behind a grassy hillock
and make my way
    through the gorse, along the edge of the fence, keeping

low, so as not to be seen.

The Spitfires are still lined up,
(although I'm SURE they've been moved closer to the gate)
and despite the number of vehicles
dotted randomly about,
the place is deserted.

Except…
    What's that
        moving
between
    the vehicles,
       slowly
    through the gloom?

I fall to the ground
scrunching up my eyes
to see through the failing light.

And coming out from
       behind a truck
is the lonely figure
of Mr Fisher.

I follow him with my eyes
and watch
as he approaches

a grass-covered mound,
a brick wall near each end,
pauses for a moment
and then disappears
from view.
Inside, it looks like.

I wait
and wait

not knowing what to do.
If he's inside the mound,
I can't exactly
watch what he's doing –
there being no windows and all.

But then something happens:
as the last of the evening sunshine
slips from the sky,
                    the long row of lights
                    that I saw on the ground before
f₁ i ᴄ k ₑ r for a moment
and then come full on.

And then it occurs to me
        (now that I know a bit more
        about electrics and all that)
that Mr Fisher may be controlling those lights

from inside his grassy mound.

And as if to prove my theory,
suddenly
a huge great **searchlight**
comes on,
close to where the mound has been lost in darkness.

It sweeps up into the sky

before slowly making its way back down.

And I know that Mr Fisher
is in charge of those lights,
although what he's doing with them,
        I have no idea.

My heart is beating fast and
I wipe my sweaty palms on my dress.
Revd Collins would have an awful lot to say about the danger
he's putting us in.
But I try not to think about that.
And I try to focus

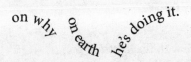
on why on earth he's doing it.

Crouching in amongst the gorse,
I watch the searchlight swoop
up and down and a c r o s s the sky,
and try to

untangle

my jumbled thoughts.

But before I can even begin
to pull them apart,
I hear
a strange mechanical
droning –

                              distant at first,
                    but getting slowly closer.

I sit up and listen more carefully,
but soon the night
comes alive with the
unmistakable noise.
Scanning the darkness above me,
I see it gliding across the heath:
          a lone Heinkel.

I can hardly breathe,
my heart beats so high in my throat.

And I'm so exposed out here with the lights:
a sitting duck,

Father would say.
I scramble to my feet,
look around for cover,
            but of course there's none –
            nothing but gorse and barbed wire.
But the Heinkel is louder and
        closer now,
filling my ears,
        a deafening din,
which somehow cannot drown
my own
        gasping,
        rasping
        fearful
        breaths.

But the explosion

everything,

            as I
                dive
                    to the ground.

My ears are ringing
and I'm sure it's all over.
It has to be.
My face is covered,
my skin is stinging,
I can taste metal,
and something hard is
digging into my eye,
but it's just

too much effort

to move.
I don't know how long
I've been here –
I really don't.

But suddenly the thought
of Mr Fisher
inside his grassy mound
makes my heart start beating
$f_o{}^x{}_t{}^r{}_ot\ d_ou_b{}^l{}_e$-$q_u{}^i{}_ck,$
jolts me upright,
and the satchel falls from my face.

I pick up the radishes
from where I've been lying
and scramble to my feet.
I've got to find him.

In front of me is a scene so different
from the one I dived away from.
The fence is down,
flames lick at the empty shells of cars,
smoke billows up and makes my eyes water.

And then I see the row of burning bonfires, sheets of flaming
canvas on fiery wooden legs.

> Thank goodness they were only dummies,
> I think.

And that's when it hits me,

Boom!

An explosion in my head,
almost as real as the blast itself.
Suddenly everything's turned

uʍop ǝpᴉsdn

and all I thought I knew
goes up in flames.

For this must be
EXACTLY
what Mr Fisher wanted!
German bombs dropped on dummy Spitfires
CANNOT BE DROPPED ON REAL ONES.

And he's been coming here
            night after night
waiting for,
            no – **inviting** –
enemy bombs
to fall on him,
            to save others.

There's a third blow,
a direct hit –

       right in the pit of my tummy –
as I remember all that I said
to Mr Fisher this morning.
And I don't think I've ever felt so sick.
Tears begin to sting my eyes
and it's not from the smoke.
I MUST get to him
and tell him just
how
sorry
I am.

Quickly, I tramp through the gorse
        to where the fence is down
and pick my way over the wire.
        It snags my ankle, but I cannot stop
and as soon as I'm clear,
        I sprint through the smoke,
        holding my satchel over my mouth,
        past the burning trucks and cars
        and clumps of crackling heather,
        to the end of the grassy mound
        where I saw him disappear,
        to where the entrance must be.

        To where the entrance
        WAS.

For all that remains

       is a heap of bricks and rubble

       and wisps of spiralling smoke,

       blocking the way in.

I sink back against

the grassy mound,

as the words I said wash over me,

over and over,

       like waves on the shore,

drowning me in guilt.

       You should be ashamed of yourself,

       for not going to fight in the war.

Over and over,

my own shame suffocates me.

       You're a coward and a shirker!

He didn't so much as complain.

And in my eyes that makes him

even more of a hero.

       How can you live with yourself,

       doing nothing each night?

And I realise with horror that
although I can be forgiven
for not being a hero
        (I am only twelve after all),
I can never live with myself
after what I've said.
Not EVER.
And I let the waves of shame
crash and **pound**
        Thud
over me
        Thud
Over and over.

Thud. **Thud. Thud.**

Like the beating of a distant drum.

More urgently now,

dull and faint

but as if someone's life depended on it.

Thud

But of course – it does!

Thud

Mr Fisher's alive!

Thud

Trapped beneath the ground

behind a whole pile of bricks,

but he's survived!

And now it's up to me to save him.

Sparks and ash flying around me,
        slipping and stumbling,
I rush round to the door in the grassy mound
        now lost
behind a pile of bricks and rubble.
The flames of a burning truck nearby
        throw angry orange light
on the scene of destruction.
        The wall (about a yard from the mound)
has taken the blast

                blocking the way in.

                        Leaving Mr Fisher trapped.

To the frantic sound of crackling and spitting,
my fingers t r e m b l i n g,
unable to grip,
I start to remove the broken bricks:

one
by
one
by one.
This, I realise in despair,
is going to take all week!

The wind changes direction,
my mouth fills with acrid smoke
and my eyes sting bitterly.
Scrunching them up,
I turn away and cough.
And when I open them,
tears streaming down my cheeks,
there in front of me,
leant against a small metal hut
is something that turns them
to tears of joy:

     a shovel.

With the shovel in my hand and
        a job   to do,

            a strange

            calm

            settles

            over

            me,
even as the clouds of dust
and ash swirl about me.
And as the pile of rubble
and shrapnel gradually
gets smaller, I realise

that I've actually got
quite good at digging.

Despite my stiff back,
my aching arms,
my bleeding hands,
my blistered palms,

despite the dust in my mouth,
the ash on my skin,
the sparks on my shoulders,
the scratches on my shin,

despite the darkness around me,
my tired muscles,
my weary eyelids,
the heavy shovel,

despite everything,
I keep going,
and going,
and going,

until the job is done.

And what kept me going was this:
the muffled thudding,
distant at first,
but ever faster and louder
like my excited heartbeat.

And as the metal door began to emerge
from behind the shrinking pile of rubble,
the desperate voice from inside
rose above the thudding and my heartbeat.
Keep going,
please keep going,
it said.

When the pile is gone,
and the ground scraped clear,
the door inches its way open
and out through the gap

s

q

u

e

e

z

e

s

the trembling figure,
and just stares at me in amazement.

And I just stare back in amazement.

For the man in front of me
is bewildered,
wide-eyed
and white-faced,

and
NOT Mr Fisher at all.

But it isn't long before
Mr Fisher

s

q

u

e

e

z

e

s

himself out
behind him.

And although he's nowhere near as white-faced,
he's suddenly just as bewildered and wide-eyed
when he spots me with my shovel.

And for a moment he seems lost for words.

When Mr Fisher does finally open his mouth,
all that comes out is
Bonnie Roberts – Mr Armstrong,
Mr Armstrong – Bonnie Roberts.
And the bewildered,
wide-eyed,
white-faced man
slowly
puts out a trembling hand
which I take in mine.
It's clammy
and his handshake
reminds me more of the way I used to clutch at Mother's hand
after I'd fallen from the apple tree,
or lost her in the village,
than of the confident way Father
(or even Ralph for that matter)
greets others.

It seems a long time before any of us speak again.
It's almost as if we've forgotten how.
The three of us just stand and stare.

But when Mr Fisher finally says,
Well, Bonnie, I don't know what to say,
I can't look anywhere
other than at my scuffed brown shoes.

I'm sorry,
I mumble.

And all the aches,
the pain,
the scratches,
the strain,
the bleeding,
the blisters,
the stiffness,
the splinters,
      everything
         I've

      fought
     against to
   carry on digging,
all comes out in one
huge flood of tears and
  I sink under the
    weight of it.

                But Mr Fisher
                lifts my chin
                and says,
There's absolutely NOTHING to be sorry for.

                You just got us out.

But everything I said – you can't forgive me for that!

> *Bonnie,* he says,
> *We all make mistakes.*
> *And how were you to know?*
> *Now, let's get you home.*

And with that, Mr Fisher speaks quietly to Mr Armstrong,
        (who is still white-faced, but nods obediently)
and leads me slowly to where
his bicycle is waiting.

> *Are you all right to sit on the saddle,*
> *while I push?* Mr Fisher asks.

I nod my weary head,
        heavy eyelids drooping
and clumsily clamber on.
        And just as Father did
when I first learnt to ride,
                he holds the bike steady,
                carefully and confidently,
                as though he's done it before.

And despite my haze of sleepiness
(or perhaps because of it)
I ask,
Do you have a child?

166

I did, Bonnie,
he replies.
I did.

A bonnie young lad
killed at Dunkirk:
Ronald—

The bicycle
w o b b l e s
slightly,
just like Mr Fisher's voice.

And I find myself saying
once more,

I'm sorry.

Sunday 18th May 1941

When at last I wake up
and open my curtains,
I see Mr Fisher
out in the vegetable patch
gazing at the potato plants.
He's wearing that faraway look
I've not seen for a while.
I put on my dress,
       go downstairs
              and silently slip out beside him.
He nods his head slightly,
but says nothing.

Everyone in the village will know what happened last night,
won't they?
I ask, at last.
And that gets his attention, fast.

What makes you think that?

Well, they would have heard the bombs! I say.
My own ears are still ringing, even now.

You'd be surprised,
       he replies.
They might've heard the blasts faintly in the distance,
but they won't have a clue from where.

168

I'm confused – where Mr Fisher works can only be four miles
to the south.

What you need to understand, he says,
is that sound only travels in straight lines.

Oh! I cry. *But there's a hill in the way!*

Exactly.
And using a piece of twine and a ridge of earth that the
potatoes are in,
he demonstrates absorption and reflection,
oscillation and attenuation.

And before long I understand what happened to all that sound.
And how no one would have known for certain that it was
coming from the heath.

Winding up the twine again,
Mr Fisher turns to me and says,
Anyway,
it's most important that the job I do
stays buried underground;
not even your parents must know.
I think you understand why.

And I don't, not really,
but I tap the side of my nose
and nod my head all the same.

Monday 19th May 1941

But it's not my parents who try to
uncover
what I've been up to.

Been doing your chicken's fighting for him?
      Barbara Robinson wants to know
      when she sees the bruises on my shins.

We told you he was bad news!
      Nancy Edwards sniggers
      looking at my scratched hands.

Betty Sanders doesn't say anything though.
      She just wrinkles her nose up in disgust
      at the dirt under my nails.

And Carol?
      Carol still doesn't even seem to care.

———

Looks like you've been in the wars,
Miss Price says,
raising an eyebrow as she
inspects me up and down
before checking my arithmetic.
And in a way, I suppose she's right.

I have been in the wars.
        And I didn't like it one bit.

Digging, Miss, I mumble.
She raises her eyes from my page of sums
and fixes them on my face, warily.
I lower mine to the floor.
For Victory, Miss.

Miss Price's red pen
is quick and firm.
Next time, Bonnie,
you'll do far better if you
show your working out.
She holds the book out to me
and it *droops* in her hand
like a   wilting plant.
I'd like to know what's going on
in that head of yours.

I don't think she would.
Not really.

━━━━━

In spelling,
I can't concentrate either.
I flick through the dictionary
until I find the word *hero*.

A man who is admired
for having done something very brave
or having achieved something great.

That makes Mr Fisher a hero, without a doubt.
He's a man who's done something very brave
every single night he's been here,
and he achieved something great on Saturday
(I mean, that bomb was meant for somewhere else, right?).
I admire him,
even if no one else
(except Mr Armstrong)
can know that he's worthy of admiration yet.

And what about Ralph?
He's a man (just)
and the whole village admires him
(even Mary Smith).
He's done something very brave by going off to fight,

but has he achieved anything great?
        And will we ever know?

And me?
Well, I felt anything but brave
on that smoke-filled, scorched hillside
as the sparks swirled around me:
small and alone and frightened.
But I cleared a pile of rubble –

hardly a great achievement in the scheme of things,
      but it was a **big** pile of rubble
      and I **did** save two lives.
And I think Mr Fisher admires me for that.
But no one else can even know,
which simply isn't fair.

Oh, and I'm not a man.

So I suppose
that means
I'm just not meant
to be a hero.

———

There's a whistling down the chimney
and a buffeting at the door,
a rattling at the window
and a breeze across the floor.

I stand at the window
and watch my handiwork
receive a battering.

Don't worry – they'll withstand it,
Mr Fisher says from behind me.
Veggies put up with far worse.

But it's not the vegetables
I'm watching.

It's Bobbie.

Bobbie,
who once stood straight and strong,
proud and tall,
ready to do her duty.

Bobbie,
who's been knocked back,
torn apart,
her stuffing gone.

Bobbie,
whose flowery dress catches the wind

like a sail

only to drag her down.

Bobbie,
who probably would have fared better
in a jacket and trousers.

Tuesday 20th May 1941

It's only just past four o'clock,
but the storm clouds above

mean we're left in the gloom

when the power turns off.
Mother thinks it's her Hoover again
and comes to find Mr Fisher straight away.
But he points outside to the overhead cable.
It's the wet leaves blowing against it,
he says.

Causing it to earth?
I ask.

Exactly.

Thursday 5ᵗʰ June 1941

> Everyone's huddled
> in the corner of the playground
> when I get to school.
> I start to hurry over, keen to be part of
> whatever it is that's going on
> but knowing full well that I won't be.
> *Wow!* Tommy Jones exclaims,
> *It's the bee's knees!* John Michael cries.
> *Can I see?* asks little Larry Kendal.

> I stand at the edge of the huddle,
> high on ᵗⁱᵖᵗᵒᵉ,
> but can't see what all the fuss is about.
> *What is it?* I ask,

but no one seems to notice I'm here.

Until the bell rings, that is,
when everyone falls silent and
moves away to line up.
That's when Carol sees me.
Her face is beaming, her head held high,
and for a split second she clearly forgets that she's not my friend
and points at the shiny red-and-white badge
pinned proudly on her dress.
She's gone and done it!
A Cog badge – here in our little village too!

But she remembers and turns away,
which I'm actually glad about (for once) –
I'd hate to have to congratulate her
after the way she's treated me,
and after I've had to keep my own achievement
        so completely hidden.

Carol's not short of admirers now.
Anyone would think she'd been
awarded the Victoria Cross.
But she hasn't been brave in the slightest.

And collecting umpteen binloads of rags
is hardly what I'd call an achievement.

But,
        for this morning at least,
it has to be said
that Carol is
our very own school hero.

        And a *girl*, at that.

And then it occurs to me,
        just as it did with Ralph,
that Carol was always a hero anyway –
        in the fights that she fought for me,
        the battles she won for me
        and the stick that she took for me.

And I never said thank you.

Not really.

———

Will you get a medal for what you've done here?
I ask Mr Fisher
as I water the potatoes.

                                   He shrugs.
                          What would I do with a medal?
                                   he asks in return.

I think of Carol's beaming face,
her head held high.
What a silly question.
Who wouldn't wear a medal with pride?

                    Mr Fisher looks at the potato plants
                                   with such intensity
                          and for such a l o n g t i m e
                    that I think he's forgotten my question.
                          Ronald was awarded a medal,
                                   he says, at last,
                          but never got to wear it.
                          It was awarded after—
                              —after he died.

I follow his gaze
to the tiny white flowers,
beginning to wilt and wither.

> *He was so young, he says,*
> *not much more than a child.*

> *And so close to being rescued, too.*

I put my hand gently on his sleeve
but can't think what to say,
so I say nothing.

> *No, Bonnie,*
> he continues, after what seems like ages.

> *One medal above our fireplace is enough.*
> *But if I can spare just one other man*
> *the pain of hearing*
> *that his son's been killed,*

> *I'll be satisfied*
> *that I've done my duty.*

And like a light coming on in my head,
I see everything clearly.

Mr Fisher's quiet ways,
his faraway looks,
his sadness,
his sense of duty.

Mr Fisher doesn't want a badge,
a medal,
admiration
or praise.

He isn't out
to make things better for himself.
He's grieving,
but doesn't want others to.

Surely that makes Mr Fisher
the very best kind of hero.

The light that comes on in my head
shines brightly on my own
selfish ambition:
I want a badge,
a medal,
admiration
and praise.
I want to be noticed.

And I am ashamed.

Friday 6th June 1941

Mr Armstrong certainly doesn't want to be noticed though
when I see him at the post office at lunch time.
I'm sticking my savings stamp into my book
when he comes in through the door
but as soon as I look up,
he seems to shrink away,
back
against
the
door
frame,
into
himself,
like a rabbit in headlights
      (as Father would say).
I recognise him immediately –
      he still looks bewildered,
            frightened and lost
as if he'd just stepped out of that bunker
onto the smoke-covered heath.

But that was three weeks ago now,
and I'm confused.

Are you all right, sir?
Old Mrs Clarke asks, concern in her voice,
as I nod good day and slip through the door.

The bell on the door c l a t t e r s noisily
so I don't get to hear his reply.

But it's clear to anyone that he's not.

═══════

I saw Mr Armstrong today,
I say as Mr Fisher and I pick peas for tea.
I steal a look at his face,
hoping that it'll give me the explanation I'm looking for.
       Nothing.
He didn't look too happy.
       Still nothing.
I was wondering if you'd had any more air raids recently?
       And still,
              nothing.

Mr Fisher's basket is full now.
He turns to examine the potato plants
and sighs.

A chap has to put up with a lot in wartime, Bonnie.
We all do.

Anyway, you know what this means, don't you?
he says, a sudden smile in his voice,
pointing at the dying flowers.

I'm not sure I do, so I shrug.
Almost time to dig up the little blighters!

And now it's my turn to sigh –
my whole body aches
                    just at the memory of digging,
and I don't know
         how
         much
         more
         it'll take.

Saturday 7th June 1941

On the village green,
the sun is shining.

Frothy heads of elderflower   dress the trees in lace
and the air itself smells sweet.
The land girls from Mr Brown's farm
dip their toes in the river
and giggle and screech while
Carol and Barbara Robinson go from door to door,
no doubt in search of rags.
Tommy Jones and his little brother
        fly around in imaginary Spitfires
clutching lumps of shrapnel,
and I even catch the faintest

glimmer of a smile

on Mrs Barker's face
as her cocker spaniel
joins in the dogfight.

The sun is shining
as I walk across the village green
with eggs for old Mrs Clarke,
but somehow –
        without friends or a brother to share it with –
I don't feel warm at all.

But as I walk slowly back the way I came,
           I am almost knocked off my feet
by an excited cocker spaniel
and an even more excited Tommy Jones.
Shoot the chicken! he cries.
Make room for the hero!

I step aside to make space
for the boys to continue their game,
but Tommy moves closer.
Chicken crony! I'm telling you –
get rid of your scrimshanker –
your brother's alive and
will want his room back!

Now Tommy Jones has always been unkind,
but he's not a liar.
Even so, I simply cannot believe what he's saying.

It's true – yer mother told us!
shouts his little brother breathlessly from ten yards behind.
You'd better go and clear out the hen house!

And, as if attempting to prove it,
they start to re-enact the whole thing for me
           (in all its gory detail).
But I don't wait to see how the story ends –
I'm off, as fast as my legs can carry me.

And when I get to the village green,
Revd Collins pats me on the back,
Mrs Clarke says, *I'm so glad, my dear!*
and even Mrs Barker beams.
The land girls all stop screeching,
look in our direction and smile.
It seems as though everyone's heard the news.
All at once the village green
seems alive and sweet and beautiful.
And the sun is really shining again.

And even though I'm clearly the last in the village to hear the
news,
Mother's still clutching the telegram when I find her.
Her face is blotchy and streaked with tears and for a dreadful
moment I think I've been told it all wrong.

But he's alive all right –
it says so in black and white.
Shot down over occupied France,
looked after by locals,
returned safely to England
and recovering in Falmouth.

Nothing else.

But for now
that's enough.

I don't mind watering the vegetables this afternoon,
nor hoeing round the seedlings,
nor pricking out the side shoots.
I don't mind pulling up the bindweed
or the nettles or the thistles.
I don't even mind searching for snails.

And when the land girls come marching down the lane
with their baskets of rations from the shop,
I listen to their song,

> Join in! Join in!
> There are jobs to be done –
> There's no need to be afraid.
> There's a war to be won,
> And who needs a gun
> When we can be armed with a spade?

And I find myself humming along.

Monday 9th June 1941

Everyone at school is at it now,
collecting rags like there's no tomorrow.
Carol's really started something – I have to give her that.
Even today's wind and rain isn't stopping them going from
door to door.
And Betty Sanders is in on it too –
> collecting fragments of fabric clearly isn't too backward
> for her then.
> Or maybe she's finally becoming one of us.

> One of *them*, I should say.
> For although my little collection has grown
> (with the help of Mother's threadbare tea towel and some
> hessian from the shed),
> I've put it away for good now
> and closed the clasps on the chest.

Of course, there's nothing to stop me going out and collecting
more –
there's no   digging or sowing or watering or weeding
to be done at the moment.
Not in this weather.

But the truth is,
today I'm not fussed
about getting a badge,
or admirers in the playground,

or standing up in assembly.
Not today.
Not anymore.

Although Carol's convinced us all
of the vital role they play,
how many rag collectors
does one small village need?

No.
I'm already playing my part
out in the vegetable patch.
It's messy,
it's modest,
it's mundane.

But it's valuable.
And I'm satisfied.

But there is **something** that would make me even more satisfied.

Ever since that telegram arrived and
switched the light back on inside,
thoughts of Mr Fisher's electrics have been
       flooding back and
          flowing round and round my head
       like a powerful current.

And soon it becomes a force I can no longer ignore.

Thursday 12th June 1941

You know I'm not supposed to know
about where you work?
I ask Mr Fisher
as we stand at the window,
watching the rain
>   snake
>   its
>   way
>   down
>   the
glass,
>   each
>   drop
>   trickling
>   slowly
>   and then suddenly gathering momentum.

I've been trying
to pluck up the courage for this
all week.

>   *Yes,*
>   he replies,
>   not taking his eyes from the window.

Well, now that I do know...
>   I falter,
>   cheeks beginning to burn,

190

…can you tell me
      what exactly it is
that you do there?

Mr Fisher keeps looking
      at the rain-streaked pane
and I wait
        for his angry reply
to strike me
      like a clap of thunder.
I've gone too far,
        I know I have.
I was told
      at the very beginning,
NO QUESTIONS.

I mean, I know you switch the lights on
from that room underground,
and I know you try to fool the enemy…
      My words run away with me
as I try to backtrack
      and remove the question
from what I've just said.

                    But Mr Fisher turns to me.
                    Would you like me to show you?
                    He asks with a smile.

And I can just make out

191

an evening rainbow
through the drops on the pane.

It'll have to be during the day –
far safer –
can't have all three of us being bombed at night.
Who'd rescue us then, eh?
Mr Fisher winked.
Saturday?

Saturday!
A seed of excitement
is sown
right in the pit of my tummy,
where straight away
it starts to take root,
twisting
and reaching
and spreading
within me,
until there's no longer room for anything else
and all I can think about
are the wires and circuits and switches and dials
inside Mr Fisher's bunker,
and finding out
just
why
exactly
PHYSICS IS USEFUL TO A HERO.

Friday 13th June 1941

Saturday!
My excitement is no longer
like a growing plant,
but it's increased so much
that it feels as though
a whole universe has begun to expand from a single atom.

Saturday 14th June 1941

When I wake up this morning,
I find that my excitement
has taken over everything.

How long until Mr Fisher wakes up
and we can go?

———

But Mr Fisher's being slower today
than Mother and Father ever used to be
on Christmas morning,
when Ralph and I would wait desperately
to open our stockings.

Doesn't he realise
just how much this means to me?
Stepping into the underground bunker,
discovering its secrets
and finding out how a real-life hero
uses physics to save lives.
Even the cockpit of a Spitfire,
a Hurricane or a Wellington
couldn't compare to this.

If only Mr Fisher would hurry up!

At last he's ready:
face washed,
nose blown,
clean shaven,
hair slicked back,
breakfast eaten,
nose blown,
trousers creased,
coat brushed,
nose blown (again)
shoes polished
>   (I've even shined them again this morning to hurry him
>   along)
and
>   finally
laces tied.

>   *Well?*
>   he says.
>   *What are you waiting for?*

———

>   I have to narrow my eyes into slits
>   as we stand in the morning sunshine

right on the ridge of the hill

>   and look down at the level expanse of heath.

The fence has been fixed
and there are a couple of new Spitfires already.
The boys from Oakmoor and the film men have been busy,
Mr Fisher says.

The film men?

Yes – they're masters of deceit,
        with all their mock-ups and film sets,
and they've never been busier than now!
        Planes to fool the enemy
        aren't so very different
        from those in the pictures, you know.

I like the idea of a film set on our heath,
but can't help wondering how the film men feel about it all,
miles from a screen,   hidden,   out of view.

                        Mr Fisher points in a sweeping motion,
                                You can't see it now,
                                but there's a line of lights
                                half a mile long
                                hidden in the heather.
                                When I switch them on
                        from the bunker control room
                        they look just like the flare path
                        you'd find on any runway.

But what's to stop our *planes*

from landing there? I ask,
imagining Ralph's horror
if he came in to land,
and found no airstrip.

> Mr Fisher sneezes and shakes his head.
> *You know – that used to happen sometimes.*

What, here?
I cry in horror,
picturing the smashed remains of Spitfires strewn all over our
heath.

> *Oh no – elsewhere.*

So there are other places
like this one?
Other places where men
invite the bombs to fall
and risk their lives,
night after night after night?

> *Don't worry!*
> Mr Fisher says, seeing my concern.
> *Now we've put a bar of red lights*
> *at each end of the flarepath,*
> *so our boys know not to land.*

> The confusion must show on my face

for he quickly adds,
They can only be seen from down low –
lower than the Germans fly.

Oh.

And there are other lights,
he says,
Dotted around
to look just like the obstruction lights
that you find on hangers and tall buildings.
And then, of course,
the navigation lights:
red, white and green
just like those on the wings of a plane.
An airfield must have aircraft on it, you see.

And come – look at this.
Mr Fisher leads me through the gate and all the way down the
slope,
across the level plain
and stops by a cloth-covered frame
about as high as my thigh
with a narrow slit on top.
Any ideas? he asks.

I shrug. *None at all.*

There's a light inside

which we switch on at night
and from the sky above
it looks just like
someone's left a skylight open.

I feel my eyes open wide.
That's ingenious! I cry.

I can't take the credit,
but yes,
Mr Fisher replies.

Oh, there's one more thing
I ought to show you out here,
says Mr Fisher,
striding towards the bunker.
I think you'll like it.

What is it?
I ask in excitement.

The scarecrow!
he says, indicating to a platform
on top of the mound.
I'm surprised,
and gaze up at where he's pointing.
But I can't see anything
except a big old car headlight
mounted on the concrete.

My very own Bobbie!

I remember the light I saw
from the bunker,
flooding over the heath,

but I can't believe for one minute
that it's there to scare off crows.

It imitates taxiing aircraft,
            Mr Fisher explains,
but we call it our scarecrow.

But why?
I ask, still confused.
You're not trying to
scare off the enemy, are you?
You want *them to bomb this place, right?*

True,
            he agrees.
But it doesn't half help to think
that they're more scared up there
than I am down here.

But Mr Fisher,
you can't be scared –
you're a hero!

Mr Fisher smiles to himself.
I was scared when I first got here, Bonnie,
afraid and adrift and alone.

I think back to the Mr Fisher
who arrived in the middle of winter
and whose eyes were distant and cold.
And I look at him now,
warm and kind and brave.
What changed that, Mr Fisher?

Well, perhaps you won't believe this, Bonnie,
but seeing your vegetables thrive and grow
has given me all the strength I need.
Nature has a way of doing that, you know.

And believe it or not, I think I do know what he means.

But even that doesn't stop the fear,
Mr Fisher continues,
when the bombs are falling like April rain.
And on Saturday night I was scared again, Bonnie.
Really, really scared.

Anyway, time to show you the bunker.

My heart is $p_ou_nd_in_g$
as we approach the bunker,
and it's not because Mr Fisher's walking fast.

The burnt-out shells of cars and trucks,
the rubble, dust and debris
take me back to where I was a week ago
and my palms begin to sweat.

But it's more than that.
        As I stand and wait
                while Mr Fisher opens the heavy metal door,
                the anticipation of what I'll discover inside –
                        the circuits and switches and knobs –
                and the secrets I'll unlock,
                leaves me almost   b r e a t h l e s s.

And still my heart is pounding.

The metal door swings open,
Mr Fisher flicks a switch
and a dim bulb tries
to throw some light
around the tin-covered room.

It's emptier than I imagined.
The arched walls are bare metal,
the floor, cold concrete.

There's a table with a telephone,
a plain wooden chair,
a toolbox,
a rusty old stove and,
in the curved ceiling,
a small wooden hatch.

It's not exactly the hero's control room I was imagining.

Cold, dark and heavy:
my insides feel like the murky room itself,
and I don't know what to say to Mr Fisher.
I turn back to face the door
so he doesn't notice my disappointment.

And that's when I see it:
a huge black board of switches,
levers, knobs and dials.
I think of the little circuit I built
all those months ago
in our sitting room,
and I wonder just how many are hidden away behind
that huge great board.
This is exactly what I hoped I'd find,
but it's far bigger
and far more complicated
than I could ever have imagined:

THE CONTROL PANEL.

It's a fairly easy job.
But we have to run a tight ship.

Mr Fisher talks me through each and every switch.
The lights he showed me earlier all have their own controls,
and need to be checked daily at dusk.
Mr Armstrong does that each day, he tells me.
You see, he arrives here mid-afternoon
and moves all the vehicles about –
that way the place looks used.

Does he know I'm here?
I ask, suddenly feeling like a trespasser
about to be caught.

It's all right, Mr Fisher says,
he knows
and, given that you rescued both of us,
he's more than happy with that.

And what's the next thing you do?

Well – it's a lot of waiting around, to be honest.
But when we receive the signal,
we switch a generator on next door,
come to the control panel
and turn on all the lights I just showed you.

And then?

If we're both around
we take it in turns to control the scarecrow –
it's easy but requires concentration.

How do you control it?
I ask.

With that handle,
he replies, turning away
and moving towards the table.

But I haven't seen enough yet.

Can you show me how it's done?
Please?

Well, it's really not all that much fun,
Mr Fisher laughs,
But all right.
The idea is to make the light look as though
it's coming from an aircraft pivoting on one wheel as it turns.
And taking hold of the handle,
he shows me how he has to rotate the scarecrow
through ninety degrees over five seconds,
switch it off for forty seconds,
and then rotate for another five
from a different direction.
Go and stand outside and watch as I do it,
if you like.

So I do.
The headlamp swivels,
then pauses,
then swivels again.
But it's hard to imagine how this fools the enemy.

Can I have a go?
I ask Mr Fisher when I return.

> *If you really want to,*
> Mr Fisher replies.

So I swivel the scarecrow,
switch off and pause,
swivel again,
and then repeat the whole process.

> *Perfect!* Mr Fisher exclaims,
> a slight croak in his voice.
> *I see I'm no longer needed here!*

It's fun! I cry. *And easy too!*

> *I'm glad you think so.*
> *But trust me,*
> *The novelty wears off after a while.*

How long do you have to do this?

I ask, still moving the handle,
but forgetting to count.

You see! he says,
winking at me.
You have to concentrate –
that's why we take turns.
We keep it up as long as necessary
until we hear a plane close overhead.

And then what do you do?

We switch off the scarecrow
and go outside to keep watch.

Outside?
The handle freezes in my hand.
When there's a plane overhead?
That's madness!

But necessary.
We need to make sure it's not one of our boys
mistaking it for Oakmoor –

sometimes they miss the bar of red lights, you see.
If they signal that they're going to land,
all our lights need to go off – and fast.

And if it isn't?

Well, then all that's left for us to do
is to take cover in here
and pray.

Us decoymen,
he continues,
are the only ones who pray
that bombs will be dropped.

And suddenly Mr Fisher's job doesn't seem quite so easy.

There's one thing I still don't quite understand,
I say, breaking the long silence that's settled over us.
How do you receive the signal in the first place?

Telephone, he says.
As soon as RAF Oakmoor
receive an air-raid warning,
they call us –
and we react double quick.

And in the event that we are attacked,
we call them to report.
Sometimes—

But I've stopped listening.
If Mr Fisher and Mr Armstrong
were in contact with the local base,
they would have been dug out

by a rescue team,
for sure.

Which means that I
wasn't actually
needed
to save
their lives
at all.

Balderdash!
cries Mr Fisher, when he's asked me what's wrong.
If you fix a leak just before the plumber arrives,
there's no doubt that you solved the problem;
if you extinguish a fire before the engine appears,
it's you who saved the building,
and if you rescue a man before his colleagues turns up –
who doubtless would have done the same –
it's you who's the hero.
However you look at it.

Wait a minute—
Did he just—

WHAT was that he called me?

When he's finished showing me the control panel,
Mr Fisher explains about the escape hatch in the ceiling.
Not much good if it gets covered by debris from the blast though,
he says, *as it did last Saturday.*

And then he leads me through a dingy corridor
and into the generator room,
where two huge tractor-like beasts
lie quietly on concrete slabs
as if waiting to be roused from sleep.

They're noisy devils when they're running,
says Mr Fisher.

Why are there two of them?
I ask.

Something I've learnt over the years, Bonnie,
he says,
is that it's always a good idea to have a back-up plan.

═══════

As we cycle back across the heather,
my mind is *whirring*
far faster than my pedals.
Like Grandfather's old zoetrope,
images flash through my mind
over and over,

until they blur together
and tell their own silent story:

    Mr Fisher operating the scarecrow,
        watching on the heath,
            praying for bombs,
                cowering as they rain from the sky.
                  Calling the aerodrome,
            finding the escape route blocked,
        waiting to be rescued,
      and realising in disbelief
    that it's me who has saved him.

    And before long,
        the images are nudged into action again
           and they're off,
                spinning round and round
                  telling their own silent story
            of secrecy,
        bravery
      and courage.

But every time,
the story ends
with Mr Fisher calling me
THE HERO.

Monday 16th June 1941

Carol's badge is still pinned proudly to her chest.
    I catch her looking at it from time to time.
But mine is tucked away deep inside,
    and it fills me with warmth.

Tuesday 17th June 1941

The sun beats down
as I fill my basket with peas,
broad beans,
lettuce,
radishes,
spinach
and chard.
Mother will be pleased.

The sunlight on my skin
matches the warmth I feel inside –
the warmth of being recognised by Mr Fisher.

But best of all,
we got a letter from Ralph this morning.
He's safe and well, has a few days' leave,
and is coming home
a week on Sunday!
Could things get any better?

Mr Fisher comes out of the house,
leans against the doorframe
and smiles into the sunshine.
I'm so glad he's my friend.

But then he wipes his brow
with the back of his hand.

213

Calm before the storm, this,
he says, looking up.

Mr Fisher goes on to explain

how warm moist air rises,

meets cooler dry air

a n d f o r m s

s t o r m c l o u d s.

But even the worst thunderstorm

can't spoil this perfect day.

Wednesday 18th June 1941

Mr Fisher was right about the storm.
It came last night,
while I was tucked up in bed
and he must have been out
      waiting on the heath,
praying for enemy planes to fly over
and bombs to fall.

But no one would have flown in that weather
and the only thing falling was the rain.
The howling and rattling woke me up
but I soon turned over
      and went back to sleep,
relieved that tonight's only enemies
were water and air,
the only possible casualties,
pumpkins and squash.

But now I'm beginning to worry,
for although Mr Fisher got home all right
      (his sodden shoes,
      which I stuffed with newspaper,
      are by the door),
he hasn't got up by the time I'm home for lunch.
And that has never happened before.

Mother doesn't fuss or complain

when his boiled egg gets cold
and his soldiers soggy.
And neither does she mention his name
(as if that were the same as asking questions,
which she's very good at not doing).

So I set off to school for afternoon lessons
past the pummelled pumpkin leaves,
the shrivelled squash,

the blackened courgettes
and the battered beans
without a word.

Just a tummy full of worry.

———

He's still not around when I get back from school,
but his shoes remain untouched,
still stuffed with newspaper,
still sodden.

I change the paper
and look all round the house,
but without any luck.
He must still be in his room.
The loose floorboard   creaks

as I hover outside his door
and a strange, weak voice calls,

Bonnie-is-that-you?

Yes, I say,
my heart beating frantically,
not sure what I should do.

Mother appears in the hallway.
I think Mr Fisher's ill, I say.
She rushes up beside me,
knocks on the door and calls to him,
Is everything all right?
Can I come in?

Yyeess, comes the slow reply
and Mother turns the handle.

Mr Fisher is lying weakly in the bed,
barely awake,
his lips blue and
his breathing shallow.
Mother places a hand on his forehead.

Go and boil the kettle, Duck, she says,
fill the hot-water bottle
and make a cup of sweet tea.

I race down the stairs as quick as I can,

put the kettle on the stove and light the gas.
Clearly the sugar ration doesn't matter today,
and that makes me worry even more –
this must be a real emergency.

The kettle takes f o r e v e r t o s i n g.
I bite my nails and drum on the table,
wishing it would hurry.

But when at last
it lets out its long low hiss
rising to a shrill whistle,
I want it to stop.

I am scared to go back upstairs
and see Mr Fisher like that
and my hands s h a k e as I screw closed
the stone bottle.

When I get back upstairs,
Mother slips it under the sheets beside him
and helps him drink small sips of tea
between coughs.

I'm going out to fetch Dr Bovingdon,
she says.
Sit with him while I'm gone, Bonnie,
and keep talking to him,
do you hear?

I nod, unable to say a word.

But that doesn't matter
because as soon as she's gone,
Mr Fisher starts talking to me.
Or trying to.

> *MrrrArmmmstrong –*
> he coughs.

> *TellMrArmstrong.*

My heart's still beating fast
and I can't think clearly,
but all of a sudden I realise
he's worried about missing work,
about putting others in danger,
and I must let Mr Armstrong know.

But I can't leave Mr Fisher here –
Mother would be furious!
And anyway, it's more important
to make sure he's safe.

It *is* more important, isn't it?
But I think of all those men at the air base,
pilots just like Ralph,
who, although they don't know it,
rely on Mr Fisher for protection.

And now I think about it, I'm not so sure

that it is more important.
Oh, what would a real hero do?

And then I think about Mother.
All the times she's sat with us,
nursed us through fevers,
through mumps and measles,
stayed calm,
kept our spirits high,
selflessly caring.

But Mr Fisher wants me to go –
selfless Mr Fisher.
He's not thinking of his own condition,
but of the men he needs to protect.

Thenumber –
can'trememberthenumber,

he quietly moans,
and his hands fumble around
on the bedside table
until he clumsily grasps a scrap of paper.
Shakily, he holds it out to me
and then sinks back against the pillows,
        exhausted.

I look at it –
a telephone number.
It'd only take me five minutes

to race to the telephone box on the village green
and back again.

Well, all right, maybe ten.
But what could really happen in that time?

I shudder at the thought.
Being here won't make a difference anyway –
there's nothing *I* can do.

But Mother said to keep talking
and she knows about such things.

I look at Mr Fisher,
pale against the pillow,
his forehead damp,
his eyes closed.

Don't worry, Mr Fisher, I say,
in a voice that's not my own.
I'll let Mr Armstrong know.

Somehow I will.

I go to the window
and look up and down the lane,
desperate
and wondering what to do for the best,
wishing that the telephone box would come to me.

But what does come to me
from down the lane
is the welcome figure of Betty Sanders,
lugging a bundle of rags.
I know she's not my friend any more,
and can't stand Mr Fisher
but it's worth a try –
ANYTHING has to be.
Quickly I open the casement,
call down
and beg her to wait
while I come to the door.

I'll be right back, Mr Fisher.
And I race out of the room
    and fly down the stairs.
        But Betty Sanders has carried on up the lane.
        I charge after her – *I've got to make a phone call,* I say.
        Can you help?
        Betty Sanders stops,
    turns rounds and looks down her nose at me
as if it'd be beneath her to answer.
No doubt she has a telephone in her own house –
I've heard that some folks do.
I can't leave Mr Fisher –
he's very sick, you see.
Will you sit with him and keep talking,
just for ten minutes?
I expect Betty Sanders will be good at this –

her being able to talk for Britain and all.

What, your **shirker?**
is all she says,
      and carries on walking.

I dig out some aniseed balls
from the depth of my pocket,
and hold them out
in the hope of convincing her,
but she turns her nose up
at my fluff-covered offerings.

And then it comes to me,
like a bulb lighting up for the very first time –
I'll give you my rag collection!

Deal,
she says.

People will do anything to earn a badge, you know.

I show Betty Sanders up to his room
and almost at once she's off,
          introducing herself,
          telling him about her life in Bristol,
          how her mother is a nurse
          and her father a doctor.
Mr Fisher's eyes flicker open and gaze at her.
          She explains that she will wait with him
          while I pop up the lane
          and that everything will be just fine.

She's a natural at this.

I creep out
and leave her talking for Britain.
Or for RAF Oakmoor at least.

═══════

I'm completely o u t o f b r e a t h

by the time I reach the telephone box.
Shakily I dial zero
and wait for the familiar
Number, please?
The digits   tumble   from my mouth,
tripping over each other
in their race to get out,
nine-seven-six-seven-one
but the operator seems to understand.

I wait while she connects me,
push in my penny
and hover my finger over button A,
anxiously waiting for the ringing to stop
and Mr Armstrong to answer.

But the ringing doesn't stop.

And Mr Armstrong doesn't answer.

There's nothing for it.

If I can't get through on the phone,

I'm simply going to have to

go to Mr Armstrong myself.

I race back to Betty Sanders
    wondering what I can say to convince her
        to stay another hour
            while I cycle up to the heath
              and back again.

And wondering how on earth I'll explain it to Mother.

But Betty Sanders pays me no attention
when I enter the room.
She's clearly in her element:
    chatting to someone
    who won't mind that he can't get a word in edgeways,
    and who can't walk away.
But what surprises me most
is that Mr Fisher seems to be listening,
and he's looking better already.

I think I like being a nurse, you know,
she says, turning to me at last.
I must take after my mother.

And it doesn't take much to convince her to stay.

———

The air is cold and
the ground is still sodden

from last night's storm.
It's not long before my socks are wet,
and my legs are caked in mud.

Feet pedalling furiously,
heart beating fast,
I ride into the wind.
But now that I'm on this familiar journey,
my mind s l o w s d o w n and I find myself wondering
just how Mr Fisher got so ill.
He was as right as rain yesterday, after all.

And with that thought, it comes to me
that perhaps being out in the rain all night (with a cold)
had something to do with it.

But Mr Fisher knew the storm was coming –
he'd told me himself.
Surely he'd have set out prepared?
He would have, wouldn't he?
He's just that kind of man.
And anyway, it is June.
Surely no one can get so very cold in June?

But as soon as I stop
up here on the lonely heath,
my arms prickle into goose bumps

and I find my teeth chattering.

And inside,
I feel
completely
numb.

———

The site seems deserted,
no nightjars
      or warblers doing their thing,
no yellowhammers
      or woodlarks
just a cold wind whipping my arms and legs,
      and a great grey heavy sky.

The gate is open and creaking slightly
and the newly made Spitfires have taken flight –
all that now remains of their wooden frames and painted
canvas covers
is strewn carelessly across the heath,
          caught in   clumps   of gorse
          and flapping in the heather.

I'm surprised that Mr Armstrong hasn't cleared it all up,
or made a start, at least.

But Mr Armstrong is nowhere to be seen either –
he must be in the bunker,
waiting patiently for dusk,
gearing himself up to save lives,
        for his duty to start.

I run down the slope,
        heart hammering in my chest.
I must let him know
that he's been left in the lurch,
that he'll be alone tonight.
If I'm quick enough
perhaps they'll send someone else
from the airbase?

But suddenly,

        I   stop   dead.

It is no wonder that
I couldn't get through on the telephone –

                the pole is down   lying flat in the heather,
        blown over in the wind,
        useless to anyone.

I race the final stretch to the bunker now with something else

to tell Mr Armstrong,
    and then
        I realise
    that he must already know.
Surely he saw it
when he arrived this afternoon?
But why isn't he out here, fixing it?
Unless,
    I think,
he's running late and isn't here yet.
I don't wait to find out,

and throw open the metal door.

Like the heath,
the bunker is deserted.
It smells of damp wool.
Everything is neatly in its place,
but for some reason
Mr Fisher's great winter overcoat
hangs on the back of the chair,
and there's a folded piece of paper on the table.
On it are the words,

Lawrence Fisher

I stand looking at it
for a long moment
while I decide on the right thing to do.

Mother would tell me not to pry
but I'm here in Mr Fisher's place,
it *is* an emergency,
and I need to know where Mr Armstrong is.

With trembling hands,
I open out the paper.
The message is short and to the point:

Lawrence,
I'm so sorry to tell you like this,
but I'm going to have to leave.
There's only so much I could put up with and
I just can't take any more.
I'm not as brave as you.
Thanks for lending me your coat,
and for everything.
Roger

Mr Armstrong has deserted.

The coward!
I think,
anger beginning to boil up inside me.
Mr Fisher is ill in bed,
worrying about letting him down and
putting others' lives at risk,
and Mr Armstrong just sneaks off
without so much as a warning
or a plan to keep them safe.

The coward!
I think,
anger rushing through my veins.
Mr Fisher gave up his coat,
willingly, I bet,
even though he was already ill,
and Mr Armstrong can't even be bothered
to return it in person.

The coward!
I think,
anger making me want to thump something.
Mr Fisher prays for bombs to fall
every
single
night,
but just one hit and a single storm
makes Mr Armstrong
give up and flee.

Coward,
I think,
banging my fists on the table.
Coward,
Coward,
and shirker!

My angry tears
                    fall
               heavily
          on Mr Fisher's coat.
I try to brush them off
but they can't make it any wetter
than it already is.
He always puts others before himself,
          I think.

But then I find myself thinking
that just one month ago
Mr Armstrong was out here,
praying for bombs to fall,
just like Mr Fisher.
And just like Mr Fisher,
he narrowly missed a direct hit
all for the sake of strangers.

And once again yesterday,
he was out doing whatever it was they had to do
in the cold and the wind and the rain,
again for the sake of strangers.

So how long must a hero
carry on being a hero
before he becomes a coward?

And what, if anything, comes between the two?

Enough!
Sitting here crying,
banging the table
and thinking
won't help anyone –
not Mr Fisher,
nor the pilots,
nor Betty Sanders,
nor Mother,
nor me.

I need to contact RAF Oakmoor
so they can send some replacement men.
And that means the pole needs to be got far enough up
so that it's no longer earthed
and the telephone can work again.

And there's no one here to do that –

no one but me.

I glance at the clock on the control panel –
a quarter past five.
That's only three-and-a-half hours 'til dusk
when the lights need testing
and the waiting begins.

I head for the door
but the chilly air makes me turn back

and throw on Mr Fisher's coat.
It's what he'd have wanted, I'm sure.
The sleeves are far too long
and the outside is soaking,
but the inside's warm and dry.

And its great weight on my shoulders
is reassuring somehow.

The telegraph pole
lies flat in a bed of heather,
the hole it was in still deep, but
earth l o o s e n e d by the storm,

now a wide gaping cavern,

its sides collapsing in on themselves.

I think of Mr Fisher in his bed –
cold, distant, motionless –
and how his tight ship

has collapsed around us.

Around me.

And I think of how I'm the only one

who can dig us out of this mess.

The hole is deep
and dark –
I've no idea
just how far it goes.
I lie on the ground and
lower in my arm,
but stretch as I might,
my fingers don't brush the bottom.

This hole is deep

and dark!
I look around for a stick,
but all I can find is a shovel
from the generator room.
I lower it in carefully,
and it dangles from my outstretched arm,
but still it doesn't touch the bottom.

This hole is deep
and dark!
Certainly deep enough
to take the pole again,
I think.

If only it weren't quite so wide.

But there's nothing to stop me filling it in –
I have a shovel after all.

And shovelling loose earth back into a hole
must be easier than digging it out.

Yes, all that needs doing
is lifting the pole,
dropping it back into the hole,
filling it in
and firming it up,
and then I'll have this tight ship
back under control.

Suddenly I feel excited and as light as air,
glad to have a plan and a purpose.
Finally, this is something I can do
which will make a real difference.
I won't get a medal
or recognition
or praise,
but I might save lives
and that,
I've learnt,
is more than enough.

My body bends to lift the pole up,
and that buoyant,
light-as-air,
floating feeling
is knocked back flat

and I come crashing to the ground.

I can't even lift it an inch.

So much for trying to save lives.
There's nothing I can do now –
nothing at all.
Trying another way is just impossible –
it simply can't be done.
I'm defeated.

I think of Mr Armstrong,
who came back here again and again;
like me, he probably wanted to do some good,
but, when it finally got too much,
he was defeated too.

I think of Mr Fisher, now lying ill in bed
defeated, not by bombs, but by wind and rain.
It happens to everyone.
I am not to blame.

But wait a minute…
Mr Fisher is weakened, yes –
but defeated?

He gave me the message
to speak to Mr Armstrong, didn't he?

He had a back-up plan,
and asked for help
when he needed it.

And help is exactly what I need now.

Carol's the one I would always have gone to for help
       but she's neither tall, nor strong
       (and nor is she my friend).
I'd say the same about Barbara Robinson
(and Nancy Edwards too, for that matter).
Betty Sanders *is* the tallest girl in the class,
       but she's nursing Mr Fisher
           and anyway, I need a doer not a talker.
Ralph is the perfect height,
     but he's all the way over in Falmouth.
Father is the strongest man I know,
      but he'll be up to his eyes with milking.
And Mother – well, I don't want to even think about what she'd
say.
       No, best to avoid home altogether.
So who else is there in the village?
       Miss Price – far too strict,
       Dr Bovingdon – far too busy,
       Revd Collins – far too old,

       Mrs Clarke – far too weak,
       Mrs Barker – far too grumpy,
       Mr Brown – Home Guard duty,

Mr Howard – well,
a conchie is
simply
out of the question.

Which only leaves the land girls at Mr Brown's.

Well, I suppose it's worth a try.

I race back to my bike
and cycle along the track through the gorse and heather
towards Mr Brown's farm
as fast as I possibly can.

It isn't long before the farm comes into view,
s_h_e_e_p d_o_t_t_i_n_g t_h_e h_i_l_l_s_i_d_e l_i_k_e d_a_i_s_i_e_s.
The sun has broken through the thick clouds now,
and their shadows lie long on the bright green grass.

There's a commotion coming from the barn
at the foot of the hill:
baaing
and bleating
and raised voices,
so I head there,
leave my bike propped up by the wall
and creep inside.

The land girls are all there
each with a sheep firmly grasped in their arms –
a tangle of green jerseys,
brown breeches,
stumpy white legs
and freshly sheared fleeces.

Sometimes they call out to each other
without raising their heads.
But they're far too busy to notice me.

I watch in amazement at their strength,
remembering the time
that Mr Brown had let me feed his lambs
and they'd bounded towards me so fast
that I'd been knocked over backwards.

I watch in amazement;
impatient to speak,
desperate to get their attention,
but utterly mesmerised
and anxious not to disturb them.

And then I notice someone else in the corner,
a stubbly, unkempt kind of man,
shearing all on his own
(and I can't say I'm surprised) –
Mr Howard, the conchie.

When one of the girls
          (who can't be much older than Ralph)
finishes her task
and lets her sheep back in its pen,
I say (in a voice that's far squeakier than my own),
Excuse me, Miss,
but I wonder if you could help me.
She looks confused that I'm here,
cocks her head to one side and
adjusts her spotty headscarf thoughtfully.
It's really important, I say,
feeling very small.
Lives may depend on it.

Another of the girls has come over,
dark haired and wary looking,
so I start to explain,
trying not to reveal too much,

but my words escape
like tangled pea stems
with no support to cling onto.

We'd love to help you if we could,
the first says with a kind smile,
but I'm not sure we'd be able to lift
a whole telegraph pole up to vertical,
even with four of us.

But you're so strong! I cry.

Not any more,
says the dark-haired girl.
Not after three hours of shearing!
And anyway, I'm famished.

By now, the other two have finished their work
and want to know what's going on,
so I start to explain again,
my words coming out even more tangled than before.
And when I've finished my story,
the first two girls are packing up their things
like they're no longer interested,
and the other two evidently think I've lost my marbles.
I'm sure it could wait 'til morning, dear,
says one whose freckled face looks friendly enough
but who clearly doesn't believe a word I've said.
It'll be dark before long, in any case.

And all at once they're heading towards the door.

                                        Wait!
                calls a deep voice from the corner of the barn,
                        and the girls turn to Mr Howard,

                surprise and anger and disgust and mistrust
                            painted all over their faces.
                                Listen to the girl!

Would you let innocent people die
on account of your supper?
Here – have mine if you're hungry.
And he offers them a small hard loaf of bread
which they turn their noses up at.

You're a fine one to speak!
spits the dark-haired girl.
Refusing to fight for your country!
Why should our brave brothers and beaus
die in your place?

I won't take up arms, that's true.
But if I can save just one husband or father or son
then I most certainly will.

And without waiting for a response,
Mr Howard walks calmly over.
What's your name, lass?

Bonnie,
I say, astonished.
It never occurred to me that he would remind me of Mr Fisher.

Bonnie here is absolutely right.
I've seen what goes on over at the heath.
I notice a lot, being alone, you see.
And it's vital that we help her,
all five of us.

Otherwise, quite simply, others will die.

The girls are looking at each other
incredulous.

Now I saw them putting those telegraph poles up,
·   Mr Howard continues,
ignoring the girls' expressions,
and I know exactly how it's done.
We'll need Mr Brown's tractor,
two planks of wood
and three lengths of rope.

Mr Brown will never let you drive his tractor,
snarls the dark-haired girl,
her hand firmly on her hip.

No, which is why I thought you could drive it,
Mr Howard replies,
without a hint of anger in his voice.
He'll be glad to have helped,
him being the Home Guard and all.

And before long,
somehow he's convinced them all
(Brenda, Joan, Sue and even Phyllis)
to join in with his plan,
whether they like it or not.

While Mr Howard gathers up rope,
>   Brenda and Joan fetch the planks of wood,
>   Phyllis finds Mr Brown's tractor,
>   Sue runs off to get the girls' coats and bikes,
>   And I try to bring to mind
>   exactly why I disliked the conchie.

Mr Howard gets back first but comes without a bike.
I ask him why he doesn't have one;
he says he can't fit it in his caravan.
So I summon up the courage to ask why he lives in a caravan
at all.

No one wants a conscientious objector in their house,
he replies.
Not even my own father.

When everyone's found what they're looking for
we meet up outside the barn.
I explain the way to Phyllis
(who still looks rather wary)
but she drives off with the planks
and we follow on behind:
us girls pedalling fast up the smooth sandy path,
too breathless to talk,
and Mr Howard flattening the bracken and moor grass as he
runs alongside,
>   jumping aside every so often
to avoid the p ^{r} i ^{c} k ^{l} y g ^{o} r ^{s} e.

When we reach the crest of the hill,
we stop   to catch our breath.
The girls all gaze in confusion and wonder

              at the sight that stretches out below us

              (even though they must have seen plenty of vehicles in
              Exeter).
I think they must have changed their mind about Mr Howard
too,
for they listen to all his instructions without one look of
disgust,
mistrust,
sneering
or horror.
Sue even pulls out a bag of liquorice twists
and offers it to him,
her freckles hidden for a moment
as her cheeks redden.

Thank you! he cries.
I haven't had liquorice for months!

There's a whole jar of it at the village store,
Sue replies,
It's not been rationed yet!

But no one sells sweets to a conchie,
he says.

Sue looks like she's about to choke
and thrusts him the whole bag.

═════

It's almost eight o'clock by the time

Mr Howard has lashed together the two planks
of wood like an extra-long bean cane frame,
Brenda and Sue have tied a rope around the pole
trailed it over the frame,
and fixed it onto the tractor,
Joan has tied another rope to the frame
and pulled it away in the opposite direction,
Phyllis has watched, her eyebrows raised the whole time,
and I've collected a big pile of loose earth and shrapnel beside
the hole.

Then we get in our positions, all in line
and Phyllis reluctantly starts to reverse the tractor
away from the frame,
tightening the rope and pulling the pole,

up, supported by Brenda,
up, up, now by Brenda and Sue,
up, up, up by Brenda, Sue and Joan.
While all the time, Mr Howard pulls the frame in the other
direction
to keep it from falling down.
And when the pole is finally upright and jerkily slides into place,
it's up to me
to dig
and shovel
and scoop
and fill
the hole around it,
while everyone stands
poised ready to let go, praying that this will do the trick.

And believe it or not, it does.

Brenda, Joan, Sue and
(would you believe?) Phyllis
do a funny little dance-like thing
and hug each other tight.
Mr Howard comes over and offers me a liquorice twist.

And all of a sudden,
the girls break into song,
out there in the fading light:

Join in! Join in!
There's a job to be done –
We all need to play our part.
There's a war to be won,
And we won't be outdone.
Join in and let's make a start!

Soon I find that I am singing along
at the top of my voice.

And it feels good.

But behind my delight
and surprise
and relief

                lurks a silent fear about Mr Fisher.

And I also feel very silly for ever thinking
that I could have done this on my own.

But all at once, I'm off
charging to the bunker
to check the line
to see if there's a dialling tone.

There is!

My heart leaps in my chest.
We've done it! I cry,
racing back to the door.
The telephone's working!

And right on cue,

night suddenly descends on the heath,

like the curtain that falls
at the end of the village talent show.

I ask Mr Howard to call RAF Oakmoor
to request a replacement
(I don't think they'd believe for one minute that I were Mr
Fisher).
But before he's even finished his question,
the officer on the other end tells him quite clearly *no* –
there can be no extra help tonight;
he'll simply be flying solo.

So just when I thought our part was over,
it seems as if *this* show
has only just started.

Wait right here!
I say,
although I needn't have bothered –
the girls are still dancing and clapping

and whooping and cheering,
and not going anywhere,
despite the dark.

But Mr Howard comes to ask me,
Do you need a hand with checking the lights?

I am astonished.
You really do know what goes on up here, don't you?
I ask.

I've watched from a distance, he says.
There's not a lot else to do in the evenings when you're all on your own.

Yes, please, I say to Mr Howard,
and together we switch on the generator
and check each light in turn,
to the utter bewilderment of Brenda
                              and Joan
                              and Sue
and the absolute horror of Phyllis.

The navigation lights come on straight away,
the red bar's shining bright,
and the obstruction lights, skylights and scarecrow
all look absolutely fine.

But   only the first two flarepath lights are working.

And that's not good.

Especially as I don't have the faintest idea what to do about it.

Come on then,
says Mr Howard
picking up the toolbox
and switching off the lights.
Let's go and fix them.
And for a wonderful moment,
I think that he has it all under control and knows just what to do.
But when we've walked across the site by torchlight
to flarepath light number three,
he turns to me and says,
So what now?
I look at him in horror.

Well, hasn't your Mr Fisher shown you what to do?

And that's when I realise that of course he has!
Wiring a circuit is a piece of cake.
All I need to do is find where the connection is broken
and fix it again:
energy source, conductor, electrical load, switch.

We scrabble around on the scrubby ground
between lights two and three
to try to find the cable.
And as soon as we do, it's very clear

it's been dragged out of line –
caught by a dummy Spitfire
in last night's storm,
as it made its first
            and only
flight across the windy heath.

Hand over hand,
I follow the cable as far as it goes,
Mr Howard pointing the torch.
And when I've found the box it needs to be connected to
I open it up, just like Mother's hoover plug
to see what needs doing.

It looks a bit different inside though
and for a moment I'm stumped.
You can do this, Bonnie! Mr Howard says.
Think – have you ever seen anything like it before?

I haven't – that's just the problem.

But then I realise that there are five other lights
each with their own connection and
we rush the hundred yards to light number four,

open up   its box

and see what needs to be done.

And after that
it really is
just like
wiring a plug.

No sooner have we got the whole flarepath working
and are back in the bunker
than the telephone rings.
My heart starts beating, double quick.
I gesture frantically to Mr Howard,
who answers with suitable *Yes, sirs.*

When he puts down the receiver,
he says,
Air-raid warning –
I assume you know what to do?

Yes, I say.
Fetch the others inside,
stay quiet and listen,
and tell me when you hear a plane.

And I switch all the lights back on,

reach for the scarecrow handle,
swivel it,
switch off and pause,
swivel again,
and then repeat the whole process
again
and again
and again.

I'm hardly aware of the others around me,

even though we're crammed into the bunker like peas in a pod,
and Phyllis has to be reminded to stop protesting.
I'm so busy concentrating and counting –
determined not to get it wrong this time.

Plane!

someone shouts,
although I couldn't tell you who,
so involved am I with the scarecrow.
But on hearing the word, I switch it off
and make straight for the door.

Brenda grabs my arm –
*Are you **mad**?*
she shouts.
You can't go out there now!
Can't you hear the plane overhead?

Yes, that's why I'm going,
I say, shaking her off
and reaching for the handle.

But the fear in her eyes
brings back the terror
of the night we were bombed –
the heat, the stench, the smoke,
the taste of metal and
the thought that all was over.

There's a lump in my throat
and my hand just won't do what's required of it.

And then Joan has her gentle hand on my shoulder
and is guiding me back to the table.
Going out there now would be suicide, she says.
And I won't have you do it.

Her voice is soothing
and it's easy to be led
away from danger
like a puppet on a string.

But Mr Howard's voice is firm
and it pulls me back the other way –
Come on, Bonnie, he says.
*We've got to do what's right
regardless of how we feel.
Show me what needs to be done
and I'll do it.*
And I find myself following him out into the night,
TERRIFIED!

We stand,
side by side,
gazing up
at the sky.

We've got to check that it's not one of our boys.
I raise my voice to make myself heard –

We wouldn't want them to crash by mistake.
But as I say it, I realise, with horror,
that Mr Fisher never told me
what the signal to land actually looks like.

So we stand,
side by side
gazing up
at the sky
waiting for
a signal
that we wouldn't recognise
and that doesn't happen.

But all of a sudden,
Mr Howard grabs my arm
and pushes me back through the door.
It's not going to land, he shouts
as he stumbles in behind me.
And there are more coming!

I know that I've got to switch some lights off,
I recall Mr Fisher telling me so.
But I can't remember
        for the life of me
which ones –
        obstruction,
        navigation,
        skylights?

The droning is deafening,
the bunker is cramped,
my brain feels fuzzy
and I just
      can't
think
     a n y m o r e .

And then

   Thud!

      Thud!

  Thud!

        Thud!

I didn't even have time to pray.

You could have got us all killed!
Phyllis shouts as she brushes herself down.
Brenda tucks a stray hair back into her headscarf
and nods in stunned agreement.
You could have let us know what we were getting into,
when we agreed to pick up a pole,
says Joan, her hands on her hips.
But Sue just turns to her friends and smiles,
I think I get what this is all about now –
and lifting that pole has made us all heroes!

Yes, I say.
That's right.
But we absolutely

        mustn't

           tell a soul.

When Mr Howard's called the base,
and got out through the escape hatch,
we gaze around us at the blazing heath
like it's our own private Guy Fawkes party.

In time, Phyllis calms down and sets off to return the tractor,
Brenda and Joan accompany me home
and Sue and Mr Howard decide to stay on in the bunker
in case of more raids
(and to share liquorice twists I expect).
I want to stay
but Mother and Father will already be livid,

and I'm desperate to see Mr Fisher –
to check he's all right
and to tell him what we've done.

On the way home,
I prepare myself for the endless questions
I'm bound to be asked
but, oddly, I'm not all that worried.
And even more oddly, when we get there,
Mother and Father aren't livid at all.
They just seem relieved to see me –
Mother wraps me up in her arms and
Father pats me gently on the head.
Brenda and Joan give them some cock-and-bull story
about Mr Brown needing help with the sheep.
That's funny, says Mother, pulling away from me,
Mr Fisher said –

      but there she stops.
      In silence.

And she doesn't ask any questions.

How is he? I ask,
my heart beating fast,
my chest feeling tight
and hardly daring to breathe.

A mild case of viral pneumonia, Dr Bovingdon says.

I don't know all of those words.
But I do know mild.
And mild is good.

He should be right as rain in a week or two,
Mother says.
As long as he stays in bed and rests.

And suddenly I can breathe again.

I'm not allowed to see him tonight:
Mother says it's too late
and he needs to rest,
so I lay awake for hours
replaying all that's happened
over
        and
              over
                  and over again.
                         And each time I tell myself the story,
                  the words change,
           the focus shifts
      and the detail increases.
But whichever way I tell it,
the ending is the same.

Thursday 19th June 1941

The version Mr Fisher gets
is the longest by far,
but tired though he is,

he listens wide-eyed

to every last word.

> And when I've finished,
> he smiles and says,
> *You see – it really is a good idea*
> *to always have a back-up plan.*

I look at him, confused.
Surely I can't be understanding right.
You mean, I stammer,
*You're telling me that **I** was your back-up plan?*

———

I'm glad that I spent forty minutes
telling Mr Fisher all that happened,
for by the time I get to school
I no longer feel such an urge to share it.
Not that I'd get a chance to,

what with Betty Sanders going on to anyone who cares to listen
(and to anyone who doesn't)

266

about how she saved the life of a man who was right at death's door,
how she's absolutely certain now that she was born to be a nurse,
and how she'll be forever indebted to this place
                              (even with our backward ways)
for giving her a vocation.

I just smile and quietly tell her to come over after school to collect her rags.
And she looks at me and listens.

———

Later in the playground,
little Larry Kendal pipes up,
But all the men are off fighting –
so whose life did you save?

That makes Betty Sanders shut up
        (something I've not seen before!).

It can't have been Revd Collins,
Larry Kendal continues,
nor Dr Bovingdon,
nor Mr Brown,
nor—

It was my Mr Fisher,

I say,
loudly,
clearly,

bravely,
for all the playground to hear.

*Your Mr Fisher, the **shirker**?*
Nancy Edwards asks.
And suddenly everything in the playground

stops –

all the games of hopscotch and skipping and marbles
and even John Michael's dogfight –
and everyone turns to look at me.

Our Mr Fisher,
I repeat.
Yes.
But I won't have you calling him a shirker.
Everyone plays their part in this war, you know.
I look around me at the wide eyes and open mouths,
but I haven't finished yet.
Some things that people do earn them medals or badges,
and I look at Carol, a light to us all,

But some things, however useful, just can't be seen
like –
    and I want to say electricity
    because of the powerful effect it has

but I know they'll just laugh –
like the things Mr Fisher does.

So, are you saying his job is Top Secret, then?
little Larry Kendal asks.
Gosh! How exciting.
*Can't we ask **any** questions?*

Absolutely not! I say.

But what's exciting to *me*
is that everyone's still listening,
no one is sniggering

and I've just fought my OWN battle
for the very first time.

———

I hand back the battery-operated bicycle lights to Carol,
Thank you, I say.
And not just for this.

Oh?
she says.

Thank you for standing up for me
all these years.
I pick at the skin beside my nail

all leathery and tough from digging.
But from now on I'm going to do it myself.

What you did back there was just the ticket,
Carol says.
What happened?

I shrug.

But deep down I know –
there's only so much you can put up with
before you just can't take any more
and you have to do something about it.

I'm sorry,
said Carol.
I really didn't want to abandon you, you know, but—

Yes, I understand,
I say,
        taking her trembling hand in mine.
And as she clutches at it tightly,
        I realise that I really do.
Please can we just be friends again?

And as if the final connection in a circuit is made,
Carol says yes, and everything gets brighter.

Things continue to get brighter still
when I get home from school.
There's a letter waiting on the mantelpiece
with an address in scrawled handwriting,
and a postmark from Falmouth.

It confirms what I expected to be true:
that my brother *is* a hero.
He *was* shot down,
but not before downing a Messerschmitt himself.
I wouldn't have expected anything less, of course.

Getting to safety was tough, he says,
but he avoided capture
and kept his head low.
He's being looked after in hospital now –
it won't be for long, he says.

And best of all, he'll see us soon.

—————

I want to visit him
in that hospital in Falmouth.

I want to hold his hand
and tell him that long before
     he took to the skies,
     defeated the enemy

and was shot down himself,
he was a hero to me.

I want to tell him that I will never again
be jealous of what he does,
wish I were him or
laugh at him
    for anything.

And I want to tell him
I miss him.

But I can't
    because Falmouth is just so far away.

———

        Digging out my rag collection,
I pick up Grandfather's old zoetrope,
wipe off the dust that's collected inside round its base
and give it a spin.

And although the chicken's still
    scrabbling on the ground,
        scratching at its hole,
           it's somehow managed to escape
        the shadow
    of the eagle
soaring overhead.

I'll never forget you, Bonnie,
Betty Sanders says
when she comes over later
with Carol, Barbara Robinson and Nancy Edwards in tow.
Thank you.

It's nothing,
I shout, raising my voice to be heard over Mother's hoovering.
And I hand over my collection of rags.

But I don't think she's heard me and
she's staring at the Hoover in disbelief.
My mother would die for one of those!
she says.

———

I lead the girls out into the garden.

I point to Bobbie,
barely visible behind the Jerusalem artichokes,
the sweetcorn
and the towering beanstalks.
You can have her dress and sack body for your collection too,
I say.
She's done her job now.

She's certainly done it well!
Betty Sanders replies,
all four of them gazing in wonder at the vegetables:
                the orderly rows of lettuce heads,
            onions standing to attention, tall and straight,
                        like sentinels,
                guarding the delicate carrots behind.

Nancy Edwards's eyes are almost popping out of her head,
like she's never seen a vegetable garden before
        (but then again, she hadn't seen cows either,
        so anything's possible).

She's protected this lot brilliantly!
says Carol, walking towards Bobbie.

                Yes, and now she deserves a rest,
                        I think,
                imagining the soft mattress
                Bobbie's ragged dress will help fill,
            providing comfort to a weary soldier.

Sunday 29th June 1941

Ralph looks dashing in his uniform
and Mary Smith is positively beaming
as she sits down beside him at the dinner table.
She cannot keep her eyes off him
as he tells us how he swam from the wreckage of his burning
Spitfire
to the northwest coast of France,
how he hid for weeks in a rat-infested barn,
how the farmer's daughter found him one morning,
how she'd plotted and planned and prepared his escape
back to Falmouth by fishing boat
and how

      without the kale and cabbage and leeks and sprouts
      growing in the farmer's vegetable patch,
he would surely have died of starvation.

———

Ralph's medal is passed around the table
for all to see,
Mr Howard included.
He looks slightly awkward when it reaches him,
like he doesn't quite know what to say.
But Father reassures him,
It's all right, old chap.
We each play our part in this, don't we?

Mother doesn't even try to hide her tears
as she takes the medal from Mr Howard
and holds it in both hands.

And as I take it,
the steam from the dish of golden potatoes

dulling its silver sparkle.
But that doesn't dampen
the feeling of admiration

inside me.

Well done,
I say,
smiling at Ralph.

———

Actually,
I wouldn't be here telling you all this,
in fact
I wouldn't be here at all
if it weren't for a real stroke of luck,
Ralph says.

Mary's eyes grow wide.

You see, he continues,
Last Wednesday night
Jerry had it in for us,
us on the base, I mean.
They were going to plaster us once and for all.

Mr Fisher's eyes grow even wider.

But do you know what?
Jerry couldn't even get that right!
You'd think with all their fancy equipment
they'd be able to read a map.
But it turns out not!

Word has it that they
only went and dropped their bombs
on some place too far south...

And before Ralph finishes his story,
I feel my eyes grow the widest of all.

Anyway,
enough about me,
Ralph says
What about you, my Bonnie little Bonbon?

Find any good hiding places lately?
I think of Mr Fisher's decoy site
hidden on the heath,
and the underground bunker
with secrets of its own.

I smile
but don't say a word.

Spotted any good planes then?
I see the Heinkel coming towards me,
and the row of blazing canvas Spitfires.
I smile
but don't say a word.

Done anything worthy of a prize then?
And for just a moment,
I'm back in that moment
frantically shovelling soil,
racing against the clock,
desperate to save lives.

And in the process,
saving my
very
own
brother.

I smile
and hold up my chin.
And I don't say a word.

Passing the buttered carrots,
Mr Fisher speaks for me,
You know what, Ralph?
I think you'll find that your 'little sister'
has just been FAR too busy

Digging for Victory.

Acknowledgements

The *Digging for Victory* seed was sown when I was teaching my Year 5 class about the Second World War and Joan Wyke very kindly shared her childhood experiences with us.
Thank you, Joan – you certainly started something that afternoon!

Without Elen Caldecott, my wonderful MA manuscript tutor, that seed would never have germinated though. You were as instrumental in helping me to find my voice as Joanna Nadin was in enabling me to refine it. I am so grateful to both of you.

Thanks also go to my writer friends who so carefully and thoughtfully helped the various drafts of this novel to grow: Dev Narvekar, Carley Lee, Izzy Smith and Andrea Fowkes among others. Most of all though, they go to Sue Howe, writer and gardener, who journeyed with Bonnie and me from the very beginning and often knew my protagonist better than I did myself. Sue, *Digging for Victory* simply could not have blossomed without you.

Early readers of this book include Ian Maitland-Round (who told me the difference between Spitfires and Hurricanes, Wellingtons and Halifaxes, and other such important historical details), Jill and Alice Penfold, Sarah Mundell and Mark Orriss. Thank you all for your kindness, encouragement and suggestions. I am also incredibly grateful to my former A-Level English teacher, Duncan Fraser, who has so generously given his time and continues to share his wisdom.

Everyone at Firefly Press has been absolutely amazing. Huge thanks go to my exceptionally talented editor, Leonie Lock, and to Penny Thomas, Amy Low, Rebecca F. John, Becka Moor and Elaine Sharples – I am so lucky to work with you all. Thank you so much for making my dream a reality. Thank you also to Harry Goldhawk for his stunning artwork.

My agent, Silvia Molteni, is simply the most wonderful agent a writer could wish for; I'm so grateful to her for appearing at just the right time. Thank you so much to Laura Caputo-Wickham for putting us in touch. I'd also like to thank Josephine Hayes for believing in me, and Luke Redfern for his continued support on my journey towards publication.

I'm incredibly grateful to my family: to Dad for reading all those stories to me as a child and to Mum for encouraging me to write poems of my own, and to both of them for their invaluable feedback on every draft of *Digging for Victory*. Thank you also to Jen, Jo and Alex whose feedback was so encouraging and helpful. Finally, I'd like to say a huge thank you to Adrian, for answering endless random wiring questions, and Christian, Toby and Rachael for putting up with so much. Reading you all the very first draft of *Digging for Victory* in our garden on the 75th anniversary of VE Day is something I will never forget.